Readers love
Tere Michaels

Who Knows the Dark

"For those wanting excitement and non-stop action with a little mystery thrown in, *Who Knows the Dark* is definitely for you."

—The Novel Approach

"That sense of the unknown and that expectation as I waited to know what came next was intense and thoroughly sucked me in. I was immersed fully into this world and plot."

—Prism Book Alliance

Groomzilla

"If you are looking for a fun read, this romantic comedy, with an emphasis on the comedy, is the book for you."

—Joyfully Jay

"As usual, Michaels infuses this book with a healthy dose of humor and heart."

—Under the Covers Book Blog

Truth & Tenderness

"Michaels brings her Faith, Love, & Devotion series to a stunning conclusion that is sure to please fans…"

—Library Journal

"The author gave us a tremendously well-written story and well-developed characters thus producing one of the best series from this genre."

—Paddylast Inc

By Tere Michaels

Groomzilla
Groomzilla & Groomzilla Does Vegas (Paperback Only Anthology)
The Heir Apparent
One Holiday Ever After (Multiple Author Anthology)
One Night Ever After (Multiple Author Anthology)

FAITH, LOVE, AND DEVOTION
Faith & Fidelity
Love & Loyalty
Duty & Devotion
Cherish & Blessed
Truth & Tenderness

THE VIGILANTE
Who Knows the Storm
Who Knows the Dark

Published by Dreamspinner Press
www.dreamspinnerpress.com

The Heir Apparent

Tere Michaels

Published by
DREAMSPINNER PRESS

5032 Capital Circle SW, Suite 2, PMB# 279, Tallahassee, FL 32305-7886 USA
www.dreamspinnerpress.com

This is a work of fiction. Names, characters, places, and incidents either are the product of author imagination or are used fictitiously, and any resemblance to actual persons, living or dead, business establishments, events, or locales is entirely coincidental.

The Heir Apparent
© 2017 Tere Michaels.

Cover Art
© 2017 Taria Reed Digital Artist.
www.TariaReed.net
Cover content is for illustrative purposes only and any person depicted on the cover is a model.

All rights reserved. This book is licensed to the original purchaser only. Duplication or distribution via any means is illegal and a violation of international copyright law, subject to criminal prosecution and upon conviction, fines, and/or imprisonment. Any eBook format cannot be legally loaned or given to others. No part of this book may be reproduced or transmitted in any form or by any means, electronic or mechanical, including photocopying, recording, or by any information storage and retrieval system, without the written permission of the Publisher, except where permitted by law. To request permission and all other inquiries, contact Dreamspinner Press, 5032 Capital Circle SW, Suite 2, PMB# 279, Tallahassee, FL 32305-7886, USA, or www.dreamspinnerpress.com.

ISBN: 978-1-64080-169-1
Digital ISBN: 978-1-64080-170-7
Library of Congress Control Number: 2017949860
Published October 2017
v. 2.0
First Edition Published by Loose Id, February 2013.

Printed in the United States of America
∞
This paper meets the requirements of
ANSI/NISO Z39.48-1992 (Permanence of Paper).

Chapter One

From the penthouse of 15 Central Park West, Henry Walker watched the sun come up from an insomniac sprawl on the floor of his bedroom. He suspected there was a Henry-shaped body indent in the plush white carpet, from all the nights he'd spent watching the New York City skyline blink over the tops of the Central Park trees. Without looking Henry knew his alarm would begin its shrill insistence in less than two minutes and his day as Norman Walker's heir would begin.

The sheets were wrapped around him, pulled off the bed when he gave up staring at the ceiling at around three. Henry timed the twist and turn, arching one long arm to slap the alarm just before it clicked to six.

Practice makes perfect.

Henry unraveled himself from the covers, rolling until he was lying in an undignified, naked, starfished heap in the middle of his bedroom floor. Not exactly the next cover of *New York Business Weekly*, but pushing back into the rug, letting himself sink a bit deeper....

... imagining sinking all the way down into the floor and hiding....

His backup alarm—all the way in the kitchen, so he had to get up—began chirping, chasing away the weirdness of his thoughts.

And so began his Tuesday, like every Tuesday before it. The cogs in the wheel of his life were turning and he had a schedule to keep.

Shower time. If he skipped conditioner, he might just have time to jerk off.

Tuesday meant his father was in the office. Tuesday meant the navy Hugo Boss with a vest and boring dove gray tie, wingtips and a pocket square that "wasn't too flashy." He ate four waffles—multigrain, no syrup, God his life was so depressing—as he stood over the sink, ignoring his beeping phone. Norman didn't text, his assistant Kit would be on the subway and the particular chime didn't signal anyone he really wanted to talk to. Jackson DeForrest III was far too much to handle before caffeine.

And that was also sad, because his act of defiance involved hiding from his own damn phone.

IN THE elevator he checked his watch (7:01) and then his office Blackberry, his iPhone cooling in his pocket, still on ignore "Jackson the insufferable bore" mode. Even with the glut of traffic plaguing Manhattan at this time of the morning, they should be able to make it across town to the office on time.

The doors opened as the elevator car reached the lobby; Henry locked his spine, lifted his chin and became Norman Henry Walker III as he stepped onto the black marble floor.

"Mr. Walker," the doorman said, tipping his ornately decorated red hat in Henry's direction.

"Good morning Carlos," Henry murmured, adjusting the strap of his leather computer bag over his shoulder.

"Car's outside sir." Carlos opened the heavy glass doors of 15 CPW onto the sidewalk.

"Marvelous."

Henry pulled his sunglasses from his pocket and snapped them on, affecting his bored rich executive look as he stepped into the May sunlight.

"Weather looks good today sir." Carlos's deference gave way to Roman's baritone as he walked alongside Henry to the end of the magically pristine carpet that led from the front door to the sidewalk.

"Glad to hear that, Roman."

An obnoxious black Hummer, washed and waxed to showroom perfection, sat at the curb as his driver walked around to open the door. The monster resembled a tank, tricked out to pretend to be appropriate for city living.

"Sir," Archie said dryly, his Ray-Bans and heavy black-suit-capped broad shoulders giving him an air of danger as he pulled on the handle.

"Archie," Henry said, politely formal. "Good day, Roman."

"Sir."

Archie slammed the door behind him and Henry took a second in the darkness, hidden behind bullet proof glass and tinted windows, to blow out a breath. A performance so artificial he expected to stumble over a director and cameras one day.

Archie got in the front seat and flicked on the overhead light in the back seat.

"Ready sir?" he asked in his monotone chauffeur "Lurch" voice, and Henry shot him the finger.

"Shut up."

Laughing, Archie checked the mirrors and pulled into traffic, heading for the offices of WalkCom International.

His morning drink waited in the holder, a giant-cupped fragrant fruity blend from the deli near Archie's apartment in the Village that Henry had taken a shine to. A warm feeling flared in his chest as Henry sipped his tea, reading the morning business dispatches as they slipped through the city.

WalkCom is reportedly aiming to post record earnings this year, despite the financial climate. The manufacturing conglomerate with energy and steel interests around the world weathered the recession in ways that can only be described as miraculous.

WalkCom CEO Norman Walker recently returned from an extended honeymoon in the Maldives with fourth wife Liberty Frank Walker. Walker is still reportedly recovering from his second heart attack last November and said to be contemplating retirement.

"When did *New York Business Weekly* become *The Enquirer?*" Henry asked, tossing the small glossy paper to the floor in disgust. The preoccupation of the press with his father's health brought all sorts of uncomfortable feelings to Henry's chest. He dusted imaginary lint off his trousers, crossing and recrossing his legs.

"Another story about the old man's ticker?" Henry could feel Archie watching him in the rearview mirror but he didn't look up.

"Yes. And more mention of that and Libby than our numbers," he grumbled. "The society pages covered the wedding—we don't need a recap every time they do a story."

"They can't figure out why you're still in business while everyone else is scrambling." Archie effortlessly changed lanes, honking at a drifting cab as he turned blew through a yellow light.

Henry blew out a breath, his slightly-too-long bangs ruffling above his eyes. "The reason is my father and they should show some respect."

"Drink your tea and relax. His majesty is in the office today and I'm sure you're wearing the wrong tie."

Archie laughed at his own joke; he laughed harder when Henry kicked his seat. Like he could feel it. Like Henry could kick hard enough to rattle the brick house that was his driver.

"You should show some respect too," he said halfheartedly.

Archie flipped him the bird for the second time.

All too soon, they pulled to the front of the pre-war Upper East Side building that housed his father's company and the only faintly relaxing part of Henry's day was over.

"Have a good day, sir," Archie murmured as Henry slid out of the back seat. "Be a good boy."

Henry twitched to sock him in the stomach but he refrained. Roughhousing in front of the guards would be—awkward.

THE GUARDS threw him routine smiles as he walked to the private elevator bank that would take him to the penthouse floor.

"Morning," he called politely, eyes quickly drifting back to the gossip rag clutched in his hand. Of course he could have just left it on the floor, let Archie toss it out, but he felt guilty any time his—friend/lover/Archie—had to clean up after him.

The crap about retirement continued to sit ill with him as he waited for the elevator to arrive. His father had only just turned sixty-two. He avoided thinking too much about the second heart attack and the implications of it—because ignoring the odds was what Norman did and Henry couldn't imagine a world his father didn't storm and bluster his way through to a successful outcome.

The elevator door slid open and the attendant—a very nice, very elderly man named Neil—nodded as he stepped inside the small cage.

"Mr. Walker," he wheezed, closing the doors and hitting the button.

"Neil," Henry said loudly, tucking the newspaper into his leather satchel. He pulled his phone from his suit pocket, checking for messages that might have piled up in the three minutes from car to office.

Can we get together tonight?

Henry scowled at the phone. It was entirely within his power to text back and let Jackson know he had no interest in seeing him. As a matter of fact, Henry would like Jackson to lose his number and forget he existed.

Of course, he didn't do that.

Impulsively, Henry hit Send and heard the connection, ringing, the pickup. A booming voice speaking over the roar of New York City traffic and Pantera blaring from the speakers.

"You realize you were just in the car. Miss me already?"

"Hardly." Which was a lie.

Neil turned around and gave him a rheumy grin.

"What's wrong?"

"David is trying to fix me up with someone…." he started, only to be cut off by Archie's snorting laughter.

"Shut up," he mumbled, ignoring another text coming through as well as the rumble of his Blackberry.

"I'm trying to imagine who David Silver, King of the Fuddyduddies, would fix you up with," Archie said. "Tax attorney? Owner of a professional lacrosse team? The human equivalent of the color beige?"

Henry tried not to snicker. "He does public relations for the Lambert Polo Club."

"Jesus Christ."

"I have to go out with him at least once, don't I? We talked on the phone and he's very… enthusiastic." Henry wanted to erase Jackson's fawning from his brain—along with a solid ten days of texts. "I don't want to be rude."

Henry heard Archie cursing another driver out then an aggressive series of honks.

"But—maybe you could do it for me."

The horn died away. "Invite him to dinner. I'll drive you. He'll be pissing himself in fear before we get to the restaurant." Archie's voice oozed smooth and sexy through the line. It reminded Henry entirely too much of when they were teenagers and his cohort-in-crime would convince him to do something against the rules. He made it all sound so delightful and so worth the consequences.

"Are you going to lay your gun on the front seat?" It sounded dirty or, at least, Henry wanted it to.

"And flex. So much flexing. That all might backfire, though. Once Beige McPolo gets a look at my… packages… you might have to beat him off. Me."

"You're an idiot. Remind me to fire you later."

The mocking laughter ended when Henry shut off his phone but he felt himself relax a hitch as the elevator dinged.

HENRY WALKED into the executive suite of WalkCom on the top floor of the building, slipping back into his serious demeanor. No chrome or glass or modern art for Norman Walker's company—no, the entire decorating scheme was hunter green and warm wood tones, gold framed scenes of picturesque English country sides and heavy oak furniture.

It looked like a barrister's office, circa 1950, as imagined by Hollywood.

Quiet-voiced staff buzzed around, dodging in out of the small kitchenette with heavy cream-colored mugs of hot caffeine. There were plenty of nods and smiles for Henry; he knew how to make friends and influence people, part natural charm and part hard core Heir to the Fortune training since birth. Not to mention they all knew one day he would be the boss.

"Morning, Maria," Henry said as he passed his father's longtime secretary. She was standing at the corner of her desk, poised to announce his approach like she was lying in wait. Her timeless navy suit and sensible shoes spoke of the time warp that was his father's company. He imagined her looking very much the same thirty-odd years ago when she started here.

"Henry." She said his name as a teacher might to a wayward but charming child. The same tone she'd been using since he was five years old.

"Is he in?" He paused, eyes flickering to the heavy double door that protected his father from the outside world.

Maria's gaze went to the enormous phone console on her desk.

"Yes but he's on the phone," she said sweetly. "Can I get you some tea while you wait?"

"No, thank you. I'll be in my office—please let me know when he's free."

Maria smiled fondly. "Yes, Henry, of course. I'll call you as soon as he's able to speak to you."

He was officially dismissed; at some point he imagined he should remind Maria he wasn't a boy in a private school uniform, eating cookies and drinking milky tea at her desk while his father finished up "one more call."

Or maybe not. That probably wouldn't happen until his father stopped treating him the same way.

With one last nod to Maria, Henry turned and walked down the small hallway next to his father's reception area. It was a corner office but it was also the smallest one on the floor, at the dead end of a hallway that housed server storage and a supply closet. The "future CEO" didn't necessarily rate something larger in his father's mind.

His father—during the long lectures on humility and paying your dues—advised him that even an heir had to earn his perks.

"Hey, Kit," Henry called as he came around the corner. The artificially apple red pixie cut popped up from beneath the awkwardly jammed desk in front of his office door—followed by the rest of his assistant.

"Morning, Henry." Kit Kelly had a piece of bagel in her mouth but managed not to choke as she greeted him.

"Any messages?"

"I went through your voice mail, so about fifty, they're on your desk. You have a ten with David, an eleven with Xavier Pense." They both made identical frowning faces at the prospect of a meeting with the senior board member or "senior blowhard" as Kit referred to him. "A twelve with the lawyers, then lunch with your father and a tactical meeting about the Medlow deal."

"Do I get to actually eat real food today?" Henry walked into his office, Kit trailing behind in her ever-present "black dress and cardigan" uniform. She hopped on one foot, wiggling into her skyscraper heels and gave only a snort as a response. His father was on a medically recommended bland diet, which meant boiled chicken and steamed carrots in the executive dining room.

"No, sorry. I'll make sure I meet you between the eleven and the twelve with a snack."

"Thanks."

Kit hit the lights—no fluorescents at WalkCom—and Henry dropped his satchel on the tiny leather visitor's chair that catty-cornered his enormous desk. The monstrosity was an antique, the workspace of a duke or an earl or something like that, a piece his father bought him for his twenty-first birthday and entrance into "the family business."

It was also impractical, the size of a Volkswagen, and Henry was saddled with it until the day he died. It was like a giant stale-smelling metaphor.

And seriously—there were eight hundred drawers. He kept losing his pens.

"Okay, let's start the day," Henry sighed as Kit ran back to her desk for a notebook and pencil.

The antique clock on his desk said eight ten. He was already behind.

"HERE." KIT shoved the napkin-wrapped hot dog at him as he half walked, half jogged down the hallway.

"Really?"

"Mmmmm, taste of New York! Most likely meat from an animal!" Kit handed him a napkin and bottle of water as she put his folders under one arm.

"No, really."

"The dining room had nothing portable and oh right, this wouldn't happen if someone would approve vending machines on this floor," Kit muttered. Her two o'clock sugar craving was a popular topic of conversation. "Your father wants you in his office ten minutes ago so your meeting with the lawyers is pushed to twelve-twenty." She veered off as the hallway split and Henry tried to eat the street vendor special without getting mustard on his six-hundred-dollar suit.

Maria was sitting down, typing away on her dinosaur-era computer. She had only recently—reluctantly—gotten rid of her typewriter.

"Henry," she said, a slight reproach in her voice as he chewed his food as quickly as he could.

He swallowed the last bite of hot dog and sucked down the water.

"Mint?" he coughed and Maria opened her top drawer. She handed him a wrapped sweet, reluctantly handing it over like she was keeping track of his sugar consumption.

"Thanks." Henry wiped his mouth, tidied his suit and checked his hair in the reflection of Maria's polished desktop.

"Go, go," she said.

Henry steeled his back and knocked at his father's door.

"Come in!"

Norman Walker was sixty-two and, Henry firmly believed, carved from the steel he sold. Anyone who looked at his father artfully colored in varying shades of gray, behind his behemoth desk, framed by sunlight and an air of determination would never for a second believe the retirement rumors. His father would give up this office the day he gave his last breath, a hundred years from now.

Henry snapped his spine perfectly straight, smiled blandly and stepped into the lion's den.

"Henry," his father intoned, not looking up from the opened folder on his desk.

He sat down quickly, in the purposely uncomfortable chair angled in front of his father's desk.

"Father."

The pleasantries ended there; they were at work and when at work, one did not introduce the sentimentality of familial relationships which made very little sense to Henry—even when they were alone, his father eschewed all outward appearances of warmth or affection. He might have remembered a hug when he graduated from Harvard.

The meeting's agenda was typed out—by Maria—and his father passed him a copy, finally looking up.

"Are you ready?" he asked and, wildly, Henry felt like that question weighed more than usual. He blinked then shook his head slightly.

"Yes, of course. We can start with the Malaysian deal."

Norman grunted in response.

And their day—like every day since Henry joined the company five years ago—began.

AN HOUR passed, then two. Henry lost his voice briefly, and knew a few points were deducted from his presentation of a potential project's analysis by getting up to fetch a glass of water from the cut crystal decanter on the bar cart.

His phone was back in his office but he knew Kit had rescheduled his afternoon yet again, curtly informing his other meetings that Henry was with Norman, which was like a *get out of meetings free* card. No one questioned it.

Henry grew hot and sweaty under his suit coat. In another world, people working this hard in a sunlit room with no air-conditioning or an open window would have stripped down to their shirts, rolled up sleeves, and discarded ties. In another world, there would be a bathroom break, more ice in the bucket, maybe caffeine.

That was not this world and Henry hadn't even unbuttoned his jacket.

Then relief—a knock at the door followed by it opening without even waiting for Norman to call out.

Only one person had balls that big.

Henry's godfather and Norman's right-hand man, David Silver, sauntered into the room, the sterling-haired picture of jocularity.

"Good God, Norman, it's a hundred degrees in here." He opened the door, leaning through to call to Maria. "Maria! Please turn on the air-conditioning." Like his initial entrance, he didn't bother to wait for a response.

Norman made a face of displeasure but David ignored him, plopping down in the second uncomfortable chair.

"Are we ready for the meeting tomorrow?"

No one at WalkCom did pleasantries.

Norman and David launched into a discussion about their meeting with potential new investors scheduled for the next day, leaving Henry to fetch David's customary three fingers of Macallan. Sometimes his job felt more like an internship.

Thirty minutes later a lull dropped into the conversation; Norman shuffled his endless pile of folders on his desk, to make sure they'd covered everything he wanted, even after scanning the agenda. This left David and Henry sitting side-by-side, and then David's grin turned devilish.

"So—did you phone Jackson?" David asked, innocent as a babe as he turned his body toward Henry.

A quick glance at his father registered little; no change to his expression as he glanced over his desk one more time, his compulsive need evident as he made sure nothing had been missed.

"We talked several times. I'm going to arrange a dinner—" Henry started.

"Not tonight. You're coming up to have dinner with Libby and I at the house."

Norman's stern voice cut through the room like a knife.

"Oh. Of course." Henry struggled to sound enthusiastic—though there was a certain sense of relief to have another excuse to avoid Jackson. "That sounds lovely."

"Well, don't keep him waiting for too long. He's a fine young man from a good family." David's ease of discussing Henry's being gay, in the open, in front of Norman, made his throat constrict as if he'd just eaten a plate of shrimp. An allergic reaction—cold sweats, airway tight, burning cheeks—to having his sexuality paraded in front of Norman. They didn't talk about this, ever.

David didn't care. David didn't have anything to lose; his money helped WalkCom exist. David's father and Henry's maternal grandfather had been close friends since childhood, and when Norman took over, it was imperative the two younger men joined forces. David to prove he was more than a legacy and Norman—well. Norman didn't come with any sort of pedigree, just brains and an intense desire to succeed. They couldn't do this without each other.

"I'll make sure it happens in the next few days," Henry murmured, feeling a trickle of sweat forming under his hair.

"Get a haircut first. Norman, how are you allowing this?" David teased, slamming his hand on the desk as he stood. "Enjoy your evening, gentlemen. I am off for the day."

"We'll pick you up tomorrow morning at eight thirty sharp," Norman said, the first words after what felt like an excruciatingly long silence. "Don't be late."

David waved, then clapped Henry on the back on his way out the door.

The quiet he left behind was brutal.

"You have more meetings," Norman said—not a question, he knew Henry's schedule before Henry did.

"Yes." Henry shifted in his seat. "Are we driving up together?"

Norman started shaking his head before Henry's question was entirely of his mouth.

"Be there by six. Libby is arranging dinner to be served at 6:20."

"Yes, sir." He waited to be dismissed—one one thousand, two one thousand, three—then got the curt nodded that signaled he could go.

Henry got all the way to the door, hand on the gold knob, before Norman spoke again.

"Make sure you schedule dinner with that… person. It would be rude to ignore David's introduction."

"Yes sir," Henry said, pushing his way out into the fresh air of freedom—such as it were—of the world outside his father's office.

Sixteen words. The closest thing to acknowledging Henry being gay he had heard from his father in over ten years.

On legs made of rubber, Henry walked back to his office in a daze.

ARCHIE BANKS pulled the SUV through the evening traffic—that unique blend of madness on the Upper East Side that included tourists, residents, and businesspeople clogging the sidewalks and filling up the restaurants that lined the affluent neighborhoods. Winter had given way to a rainy April and now an unseasonably hot May, and no one was eager to be inside. Archie parked illegally in front of the WalkCom building, tossing a wave through the window at the meter maid patrolling the area.

She gave him a flirty smile. And didn't make him move.

Henry had texted earlier—the day was being cut short, but no explanation as to why. The console clock read 4:55; he never expected Henry to be early, so he cranked the Metallica and the air-conditioning, and loosened his tie. He anticipated a quick end-of-the-day trip—drop Henry off, go home to get ready for dinner with his mother, make dinner with his mother *on time*, then home before ten to finish his homework. Tomorrow morning his start time was early due to a business meeting in Westchester.

Which meant Mr. Walker would be gracing him with his presence. He had to remember to dust the back seat—and make sure there was Mozart, not Metallica playing when he opened the door.

Mr. Walker's only son, Henry, was far less high maintenance. Also, Archie had never blown the senior Mr. Walker in the parking garage at the Met.

Good times, good times. Henry and champagne usually ended in a very good time. Archie had filched several high-quality examples of the bubbly from the estate wine cellar for that very purpose.

Archie dug out the book he was reading—*Love in the Time of Cholera*—for one of his three online classes, and flipped the worn paperback to chapter ten. Fiction wasn't something he generally had time for, and his business degree didn't stress the importance of magical realism, but sometimes there were limited options when it came to class selection. Then again, it didn't matter—not anymore. For the first time in six years, there was no "next semester." A few short weeks, one last push, and he was done.

Soon he'd have a job that didn't require a gun permit and a uniform.

The job hunt began months ago, with Archie sending out applications and letters to the myriad of companies in New York City. There were a few interviews and even fewer second ones but to his great joy, Ferelli and Sons had called him back for a third meeting, day after tomorrow.

This was a chance to fly the coop, go somewhere no one expected him to open a door or beat the rush hour traffic on an airport run. Ferelli and Sons ran a small importing company, and they were looking to expand their operations into Asia. Most importantly, they didn't do business with WalkCom so Archie felt like this was his chance to start a new life. He had been waiting so long for this opportunity. He could taste the welcome change.

Wonderful and terrifying all at once—WalkCom had been signing his paychecks since he was seventeen, and while it was hardly his life's dream to caretake rich people, it was home in so many ways.

It was also where Henry was. All his excitement always felt tempered by the reality that wherever he went, Henry wouldn't be there.

His phone buzzed a few minutes later. Henry's signal that he was on his way down, and Archie now had a part to play.

He straightened his suit jacket—specially tailored to fit his broad shoulders and six-foot-five-inch frame—and readjusted his tie. He slid his black sunglasses into place to hide his amused gaze, and he exited the driver's-side door with an exaggerated stretch of his muscular body.

Some bodyguards got by blending into the background for the element of surprise. Archie preferred to flash his brawn right up front.

He walked to the opposite side of the vehicle, leaning against the door with a dangerous air, a flexing of his muscles under the heavy weight of his suit. People skittering along the sidewalk generally didn't notice him, but a few tourists flashed him alarmed expressions.

Archie Banks looked scary as shit.

Henry came flying out the front doors a second later, blond hair slightly too long and in his eyes as he hustled to the car like the hounds of hell were on his heels. Archie went into chauffeur mode, opening the back door with a sharp jerk as Henry got close.

His boss gave him a solid eye roll as he walked by.

"Ah-nuld."

"Oh, that joke never gets old." Archie sighed as he slammed the door, narrowly missing Henry's wingtips.

"Congrats on the half day. Home?" Archie asked when he got into the front seat, locking the doors and lowering the epic beats of "Enter Sandman" before Henry died from having real music inflicted on his ears.

"Unfortunately not. Apparently I am required to attend dinner with Norman and Libby." Henry sounded anything but enthused, and Archie checked the dash.

"Are we waiting for your father?" He felt a slight panic—this wasn't his best tie, and he was sure the back seat could use a vacuuming.

"No. Norman is taking the other car, and we're supposed to meet him up there," Henry said. "Let's stop and pick up some wine. Maybe flowers?"

"Not a problem." Archie pulled away from the curb. "You need to change first?"

"Why? Do I look rumpled or something?" Henry's eyebrows formed a snooty upside-down vee, which Archie found strangely attractive as he watched in the rearview mirror.

"Actually you do." Archie had a split-second annoyance he couldn't think of a better insult. Damn it. "His Majesty isn't going to put on the air-conditioning until someone actually dissolves into a puddle of water so you might want to wear less clothing to the office for a while."

Henry sighed dramatically scrubbing his face. "Fine, drop me off at my apartment, and if you could grab the wine and flowers, and pick me up when you're done that would help. It shouldn't make us too late."

Archie nodded, cutting through the swarms of cabs and commuters to get into the left lane.

"Are you staying over at the house, or am I waiting?" Archie made a quick right as soon as the light turned green, heading toward West End Avenue, where Henry's apartment building was.

"Staying over I assume." Henry flashed him a frown in the mirror. "Is that going to cause you any problems?"

Archie didn't say anything. It would wreak a bit of havoc with his schedule, in addition to breaking yet another dinner date with his mother and delay his interview prep until tomorrow since he didn't have time to run home and grab his laptop. Again. "My hours are what you decide they are," he said finally.

"That isn't what I asked."

"I'll eat dinner with Magnus, then finish my book." He shrugged, settling quickly into a more formal tone.

"That isn't an answer," Henry muttered, looking out the window with the frown still in place.

Archie rolled his eyes; he had never been good at ignoring Henry when he was sulking theatrically. Not when they were children together, and not now.

"It's fine—you owe me," Archie teased, his voice gentle.

A small smile crawled across Henry's mouth as their gazes met in the rearview mirror.

"Whatever you want," Henry murmured. He licked his lips slowly.

Archie managed to keep the Hummer off the sidewalk.

"Deal. Now stop frowning. You only have a few good years of wrinkle-free skin left," Archie said with a smirk.

"Duly noted." But Henry was definitely pleased as he swiped his phone open and began scrolling.

ARCHIE SWUNG around and idled at the entrance of the building. There were three bottles of Chateau Malescot St. Exupery in the portable cooler on the floor of the front seat and two-dozen purple hydrangeas wrapped in green paper laid neatly next to him. He lowered the volume on the Pantera flooding the Hummer with sound.

He checked the dashboard clock and picked up his phone. His mother would be back from physical therapy by now, and he needed to break the news that he wouldn't be home for dinner.

Again.

"'Lo?"

"Mum, it's Archie."

Evelyn Banks went from those strong, reserved British tones to a delighted coo in ten seconds flat. Long years of answering another family's phones as an employee gave her quite the artificial affectation—until she knew it was her pride and joy calling. And since Mr. Walker had hired a fellow Brit for a reason, she made sure to never lose a speck of her accent.

"Archie, darling. I just got home, but I have beef and potatoes in the cooker for you."

He could hear her shuffling about the small kitchen of her Brooklyn apartment, the tap of her cane and the drag of her leg against the floor. All the arguing in the world couldn't convince her to come live with him in the city after her stroke; she liked her freedom, and she also liked pretending Archie needed his privacy for relationships.

If she only knew.

Archie closed his eyes, tried to school his voice into something other than resigned.

"That sounds delicious," he said gently. "But I'm afraid I have to work tonight, Mum. Can I come and have a late lunch with you tomorrow instead?"

He caught the sigh under her breath.

"Of course, my love. You just ring up when you're on your way, and I'll warm it up," she said, familiar false cheer and all. "Are you going up to the house, then?"

"Yes. Henry has dinner with Mr. and Mrs. Walker." The formality drilled into him during his youth slipped into his voice. "We're heading up shortly."

"Ah well. Understandable, duty calls." Evelyn knew all too well. "Say hello to Magnus for me. I haven't seen him in an age."

"Will do." Archie sat up from his sprawl, looking quickly at the entrance. Like a sixth sense, he realized he needed to get back to work. "Listen, I have to go, Mum—Henry's coming."

"Say hello to him too," his mother said drily. "Tell him I'll bake his favorite apple tarts if he lets my boy have a day off now and again."

"Yes, Mum." Archie laughed. "Love you."

"Love you too, Archie. See you tomorrow."

Archie switched off the phone and tucked it away in the console. An adjustment to his tie and he was out the door to meet Henry on the sidewalk.

"Get everything?" Henry asked, shifting his bags. He handed Archie his overnight bag, then hooked the suit bag inside the vehicle himself.

"All set. We should get going." Archie opened the door, inwardly cringing as he realized he didn't have his shaving kit. There was an extra suit up at the house, but still—it sucked to be without basic comfort items.

"It's in my bag, your extra kit," Henry murmured as he got into the back seat, his voice pitched low even though there was no one around to hear him. "I know you didn't have a chance to go home."

"Oh—thanks." Archie flushed a bit, embarrassed—and pleased—at Henry's thoughtful gesture. They weren't like that, doing things as a couple would. Because they were not a couple, despite his kit being in Henry's apartment. And maybe a spare uniform. He didn't let himself think that way, and he assumed Henry did the same.

"No problem. You'll be driving Norman tomorrow, and no one wants a spot inspection to go badly," he teased, flashing his gorgeous smile as Archie shut the door.

No, no one wanted that.

HENRY LEANED against the posh leather seats, trying to relax after the hectic rush of his day. The brief moment with his father stuck with him. His father encouraging him to set up a date with Jackson could be about appearances. Or maybe….

Dare he reignite that dream from his youth when he thought his father might come around? He might understand his father's formality—his knight's armor against the rest of the world that looked down on a man who married his way into his position. He might understand the rigidity—the airs he kept to reinforce that he belonged among all that old money. He wanted Henry to be strong and prepared and impervious to whatever his enemies might throw his way.

But Henry was still a human being who longed for his father to *see* him. Really see him, outside this cage of inheritance.

So he joined the firm and waited, worked hard and waited. Sat at his father's bedside and waited. At some point he'd have to reevaluate what was waiting and what was a stubborn refusal to see the facts.

But the fact remained that Norman had been acting strangely for weeks, little slips and bits of time when he seemed weirdly out of character and Henry was starting to feel paranoid and unsettled by his father's behavior. Could he possibly be fooling himself about Norman's state of health? Maybe he could steal a minute to speak to his stepmother, inquire about his well-being.

"You're quiet," Archie said, pulling him out of his brooding.

"Sorry—too much on my mind."

"Ah, so a day ending in *y*."

They both laughed, a memory shared from their childhood, when Magnus, the butler, would conclude the regular recitation of their bad deeds with that phrase.

"There's a lot going on before the board meeting and this meeting tomorrow. And Father is hinting at a trip to Japan in July." Not wanting to confess his fears out loud, Henry checked his messages again; Kit had promised to forward some research on the company they were trying to buy in Thailand.

"July?"

Henry looked up; Archie's shoulders had crept up a notch, and his voice held an odd note.

"What?"

"I'm…." Archie paused, and his awkwardness dropped something unpleasant in Henry's stomach. A realization.

"You're interviewing for jobs, of course." The cool tone, the precise enunciation; when one is uncomfortable, one must not sound uncomfortable.

Of course that worked better with people who didn't read you like a book.

"Yes, I'm interviewing. I realize I can't make demands when it comes to my job duties, but…."

"You don't have to come." Petulance that made him angry with himself. It wasn't Archie's fault he was taking advantage of the opportunities at his feet.

Archie sighed. "Yes, I do. If your father insists on it."

Henry swallowed but didn't answer; he could feel a faint sweat popping onto his skin.

"You need to start interviewing someone to replace me."

Words so loaded that the second they were spoken, the entire car seemed to fill with dread and gloom. Henry felt his throat tighten.

"I'll have Human Resources get right on that," he snapped.

Archie held his gaze in the mirror briefly, then turned his attention back to the road.

The rest of the ride was tense, awful silence; a balloon of reality popped and Henry felt a rush of shame—and the pressure of time ticking away.

All the lights were on as they pulled around to the front of the Tudor mansion Henry had grown up in. The graveled, circular driveway crunched under the wheels of the Hummer as they parked near the hedged lily pond at the base of the main stairs.

Norman and Libby were waiting, clearly alerted by the alarm system when the car had passed through the front gates a mile down the road.

"Son," Norman called as Archie opened the door and Henry stepped out.

"Father. Libby." Henry hurried up the walk and stairs to kiss Libby on the cheek. She was perfectly turned out in a black skirt and cream twinset, her raven black hair tied back like a prim schoolmarm's.

"I've missed you," his stepmother said sweetly, clasping Norman's hand tightly. "We have lovely gifts from our trip for you."

"Looking forward to hearing all about it." Henry tucked his hands behind his back.

"Let's go, then. Dinner will be ready shortly. Archie?" Norman was leaning around Henry, still neat as a pin in his work suit. "Bring Henry's bags up to his room, and then you can park the car."

"Yes, sir." Archie was back at the Hummer, his voice smooth, and Henry resisted the urge to turn around.

"Oh wait, forgot something," Henry said, turning and then hurrying down the steps.

Archie was standing at attention, his blue eyes cool and not at all looking in Henry's direction.

"The flowers and the wine," Henry said quietly, aware his father and stepmother were watching as he stopped at an appropriate distance from his lover.

"Front seat," Archie intoned; he was already moving. "Allow me."

Henry took a deep breath and followed Archie around the other side of the Hummer, affording them a bit of privacy in the dusk.

Archie was pulling the wine out of the cooler and tucking it into a handled tote bag. Henry allowed himself a second of madness to touch his fingers to Archie's wrist.

"I'll come to the pool house," he murmured, noting the way Archie stiffened at his words. "Father and Libby will be in bed by ten. I'll come down."

Archie gave him a penetrating glare, a look that seemed to register in Henry's bones. "How positively *Masterpiece Theatre*, Henry—you meeting the help under the cover of darkness after his lordship is asleep," Archie muttered.

"Leave a bottle in there. Bring it in with you." Henry kept talking, ignoring Archie's snipe.

Archie didn't say anything, but he left a bottle of wine in the cooler, closing it with a heavy thunk.

Relieved, Henry collected the bag with the wine and the bouquet of flowers. Without another word, he walked quickly back to where Norman and Libby were waiting.

"Sorry—these are for you." Henry handed Libby the flowers. "I have wine for dinner."

"We've already got a bottle opened." Norman turned to head back into the house.

Libby held back, her smile pleased as she took Henry's arm.

"You're very sweet. These flowers are beautiful—and purple, my favorite."

They walked into the house, trailing behind Norman as he nodded to the stiff-necked butler who waited like a sentry in the grand foyer.

"Mr. Walker."

"Magnus."

The white-haired butler was a relic of another time, another world; he predated even Norman in this house. At this point no one was sure of his actual age, and no one—no one—dared ask. He barely came up to Henry's shoulder, his squat form stuffed into his ever-present black suit, more wiry white hair in his eyebrows than on his head.

"Could you please give these to Hilary, put them in some water?" Libby asked, handing the bouquet to Magnus.

"Yes, madam. Dinner will be ready in ten minutes."

"Perfect timing, thank you."

They continued on, still arm in arm, and Henry wondered if Magnus and the staff thought his and Libby's relationship oddly intimate. He assumed they all thought he was straight. Or maybe, like his father, they didn't find it a topic of polite conversation.

"How was the drive?"

"Uneventful. Some traffic," Henry said. *My only real friend is leaving soon, and I don't know what to say or do about it. We also sleep together a fair amount, so it's also like I'm losing the only person who truly knows me.*

The drawing room loomed ahead. Norman stood at the glowing fireplace, drinking his usual scotch from a square-cut glass tumbler. Bland diet aside, nothing came between Norman and his evening drink.

The crystal chandelier overhead threw just enough light for Henry to make out the monoliths of his childhood; the leather sofa and soft chocolate-colored velvet wing chairs, the low walnut tables and crystal lamps. Henry knew his mother had decorated this room for his father soon after they married, and nothing, not a single thing, had been changed from her initial work, even as the rest of the house underwent a makeover with every new Mrs. Walker.

This room, however, was a twenty-three-year-old memorial.

"Oh dear, I forgot to tell Archie to get dinner in the kitchen," Libby said, letting go of Henry to walk to the bar.

"He grew up here. He knows where the kitchen is." Norman gestured with his drink toward Henry. "Something to drink?"

"No, thank you." Henry sat on the sofa, back straight and shoulders relaxed. "That's very kind of you, really. But Father is right. If Archie forgets to come for dinner, Magnus will send someone around to get him. They won't let him starve."

"Right, of course. I forget sometimes that he's always been a fixture around here. He's so quiet and serious—was he like that as a boy?" Libby chattered, her tone just slightly nervous as she perched on a chair close to Norman, sending him furtive looks.

Henry got lost in his thoughts, remembering running helter-skelter through the property with Archie, getting far too dirty for Henry's nanny's liking. For all the scolding and threats to tell his father, no one had ever ratted them out—not even when they brought home garter snakes in their shorts after an epic day of "safari-ing" near the marshes and "accidentally" set them loose in the library. The staff liked Henry, and they didn't necessarily agree with Norman's stern parenting rules. Since he was seldom there, they tended to defer to what Camille would have wanted—letting Henry be a child.

"Oh God, no. Archie was quite the rogue. Always dragging Henry into some mess. But he grew out of it. His mother's influence, clearly." There was almost something… fond… in his tone. But that changed when he spoke again. "Thankfully, the boy didn't end up like his father."

"Philip's dead, Father. We shouldn't talk badly about him," Henry said quietly, looking down at his shoes. Archie despised his father and would probably agree, but it still felt wrong.

"Deadbeat and a gambler." Norman sipped his drink after his last words. "But no matter. Archie has proven himself an excellent young man. I'll be sorry when he leaves."

Henry sat up a bit straighter.

"Leaves?" Libby asked.

"He's nearly done with his degree. I would assume he'll be heading off for a proper job when he's through."

Libby sat down on the sofa next to Henry. "What's his degree in?"

"International business," Henry said absently.

"Well, in that case, WalkCom should be the first one offering him a job," Libby said with a laugh. "I assume he has good grades."

"Four point oh."

Libby gave her stepson a curious sideways glance. "Of course. He's a very smart man. Norman, why don't you see if you have a place for him at the company?"

If his father were capable of rolling his eyes, he absolutely would have but instead maintained polite control. "My dear, that is a kind thought. But it wouldn't look right—elevating him like that." Henry felt his father's gaze on him as if he was waiting for a reaction.

Henry held his tongue.

Libby's face squinched up. "Elevating…." She shook her head. "He's smart and loyal, and he must know a thousand things already about the business considering he's been here all his life."

Henry wished he had the nerve to point out that his father had come from nothing and ended up being handed a billion-dollar company by marrying Camille, but their relationship didn't work like that, and Norman had been playing lord of the manor for so long he had apparently forgotten his humble beginnings in Dorchester and then a Brooklyn walk-up, and only his degree from Baruch wasn't honorary.

Despite the fact that Archie was more like Norman than Henry himself, Norman would never see him outside his own narrow perception—a young man forced to take a job as a chauffeur to pay off his father's debts. Blue collar and not "one of them."

"You're very sweet, Libby," Henry said, quiet and resigned. "But I doubt Archie would accept an offer like that. He'll want to be somewhere to start fresh, a company where no one knew of his days as a chauffeur."

Libby—who had come from nothing to be a highly regarded interior designer—clearly didn't like that answer, but nonetheless she understood it, because she nodded as he spoke.

"You're right," she said. "I hope at least you can at least offer him an excellent recommendation."

"Of course." Norman finished up his drink. "Henry will make sure Archie has what he needs as he moves on. I doubt it will take him long to find a position." He checked his watch. "Henry, you should stay in touch with him. He could prove to be a valuable contact in the future."

"Dinner should be ready," Libby said suddenly, standing up and clapping her hands together. "Let's go, then."

Henry remained on the couch, even as Norman and Libby headed out the door toward the dining room. Once the shock of his father's complimentary words about Archie died off, his head swirled with the reality and the inevitability of Archie not being a daily fixture in Henry's life.

The heaviness settled over him like a fog.

Chapter Two

Hilary served dinner as soon as they sat down: three courses of bland, healthy food that made Henry long for Mrs. Banks' shepherd's pie with an almost physical ache. Thinking of her made him think about Archie, of course, and that made dinner increasing longer and harder to deal with.

He could say something, of course. To Archie. Tell him that once he finished his degree and found a position elsewhere they could keep seeing each other. As friends and—more.

In secret, still. Because the publicity of Henry dating his former bodyguard and driver—Norman wouldn't allow it. His father didn't bring up marriage or children, even with Henry turning thirty in just a few years. But even unspoken, it was loud and clear—Henry's inheritance required an heir.

Maybe that's why he was encouraging Henry's contact with Jackson. If he had to accept Henry was gay, at least he could get a socially connected son-in-law in the deal. His stomach curled with displeasure at it all.

Or maybe he could just say fuck it and quit, follow Archie into the world, and figure out his own path. But even as that thought made him feel empowered for a split second, he knew it would mean leaving behind the legacy mapped out for him by not only Norman, but his late mother Camille and his grandfather. *Some day this all will be yours* was a paralyzing, weighty gift.

Henry picked through the salmon and poked at the steamed zucchini. Four bites through and he was on his second glass of wine, his collar too tight and his posture less than perfect. Fortunately Libby chattered about the Maldives and some art installation fundraiser through until dessert, without Henry having to contribute much.

When Hilary returned with an angel food cake and fresh fruit, Henry sighed a little too loudly.

"Henry, is there something wrong?" Norman asked, his tone an audible memory of years gone by. *Sit up straight, mind your manners, remember who you are.*

"No, no. I'm sorry." Henry smiled and shook his head. "Long day, thinking too much about work I suppose."

Norman frowned, moving slightly in his chair to allow Hilary access to his plate.

"I appreciate your concentration on the company but we're eating dinner now and it undoubtedly hurts Libby's feelings to know you're not listening to her." He nodded as Hilary spooned some strawberries on his cake. "Thank you, Hilary."

The older woman moved around the table to Libby's plate. She gave Henry a little smile as she leaned over.

"Thank you, Hilary, it looks wonderful," Libby was saying. "And Norman's right—you need to relax, Henry."

"Of course, my apologies." Henry drank some more wine, eyes on the cream linen of the tablecloth until Hilary came to serve him dessert.

"Norman, I was thinking we should have a little get together next weekend since we're back. Just a few of the neighbors," Libby said and Henry took the opportunity of his father's noncommittal grunts to murmur something to the housekeeper.

"I'm sorry, Hilary, truly. But if I don't get some real food the buck's head on the study wall is going to start looking edible," he whispered and Hilary—bless her—stifled a laugh.

"Saved you a plate of stew and some cake in the kitchen," she whispered back.

"You're the best. I'll come get it in a bit."

Hilary straightened up and left the dining room, as Libby continued to cajole Norman into a party.

"You'll come, won't you, Henry?" She asked brightly.

"Of course," Henry said, quickly shoving some tasteless spongy cake in his mouth.

MAGNUS AND Archie ate in the kitchen, perched on high stools around the heavy wooden table tucked in the back of the enormous space. Hilary joined them after dessert was served in the main dining room, bringing with her a bottle of white wine from the small refrigerator in her room.

"Well, what's the occasion then?" Magnus asked, between spoonfuls of Hilary's delicious country stew.

"No occasion, just a need," Hilary said dryly, settling down between the two men.

"They've been gone so long—must've be nice with the quiet." Archie took it upon himself to open the bottle—a handy screw top—and pour a healthy amount in each of their mismatched empty water glasses.

"Oh, it was heaven. I got all the inventory done, restocked the pantry and the wine cellar, did my spring cleaning." Hilary took a sip of the wine and sighed contentedly. "Like a vacation."

"I realize it's been a while but I'm pretty sure a vacation doesn't involve vacuuming under the beds," Archie teased, tearing off a hunk of sourdough bread to dip into the rich gravy.

Magnus chuckled.

"I put my feet up a few times but the quiet was nice," Hilary said firmly. She laid a napkin across her conservative navy skirt. "Mrs. Walker is lovely but I'm not sure Mr. Walker is used to me yet."

"It's only been a year," Magnus reminded her as he raised his glass to her. "You made it past probation—it'll be fine."

"True." Hilary didn't look convinced, concern flitting over her attractive face. "I'm afraid I'll never live up to your mom, Archie."

Archie smiled, dabbing his face with his napkin. "My mum is a force of nature and I am devoted to her skills as a housekeeper and cook but honestly, Hilary—you're doing great. If you weren't, you would have been gone already."

"Blunt," Hilary laughed, picking up her spoon.

"You might have noticed, Mr. Walker runs on first impressions and changing his mind is like changing the pattern of a hurricane."

"Oh, I noticed." She tucked into her dinner. "And he enjoyed dinner tonight…." her voice trailed off and she stifled a laugh.

"What?" Archie asked, fully immersed in his bowl of stew and glass of wine.

"Nothing just—Henry could barely choke down that meal. You know—I can't use any salt or seasonings. I told him I left real food for him in the pantry." Hilary couldn't stop smiling as she filled her spoon with stew.

Archie grinned, shared a glance with Magnus. "See, Hilary, you are perfect for this job. The staff has been feeding Henry on the side since he was a toddler."

"Yer mother was a master of making two meals and Mr. Walker never being the wiser," Magnus laughed, loud and clearly amused as he poured himself a second glass of wine. "Evelyn thought it a crime that boy wasn't allowed sweets."

"An edict she broke often," Archie said softly. There were so many memories, good and bad, in this kitchen; it was hard to separate them out from each other.

His mother baking biscuits and hiding them in the big jar at the bottom of the pantry. He and Henry doling out their allowed two a day, sharing their treats in their various hiding places; the oak tree by the back gate, the abandoned stone barn in the far corner of the property.

"Evelyn has a gentle heart." Magnus's tone was affectionate. "She just wanted to mother Henry after the first Mrs. Walker passed."

"How did she…." Hilary started then shook her head. "Sorry."

Magnus sighed, clinking his glass against the edge of his plate as he set it down.

"Aneurysm," the elderly man said, pushing his plate away. "Henry was three, nearly four? Mr. Walker was in Japan on a business trip. Terrible time, just awful. The nanny—Mrs. O'Malley, dreadful woman—she minded Henry until Mr. Walker came home and even then. Well. Hard to bury your wife and take care of a little boy and manage a business," Magnus said diplomatically. "Terrible times."

Archie hated that version of the story. His mother had only been working at the house for six months when Camille Walker died. She was an assistant cook, trying to earn enough money to support Archie and his perpetually unemployed father. In the ten months between her hiring and Archie and Philip arriving at the house to live, his mother had advanced to housekeeper and made Henry's well-being her mission.

"Be nice to the little boy," she told Archie. "His mum went to live with God in heaven and he's lonely." He was five and found the prospect of never seeing one's mother again to be positively horrifying. So he made Henry his responsibility, from tying his shoes to getting him to smile at least once a day.

Later—making friends at the local high school and interacting with other people outside the estate—he would realize how horribly dysfunctional this household was, with Mr. Walker's inability to keep his large staff due to his ridiculous rules and what amounted to neglect of his only child as he threw himself into building the newly renamed WalkCom to greater heights. Mrs. O'Malley was stealing from him, the head housekeeper was a drunk—and Evelyn Banks did not have the ability to walk away from the mess of it all with an innocent child sitting in the midst of it.

"That's awful," Hilary said, dismayed at Magnus's story. "How sad."

"Ah, but Henry turned out wonderfully. And hopefully the new Mrs. Walker will prove to be as kind as she appears to be," he said. More diplomacy. The second and third Mrs. Walkers had been utter nightmares, with more staff turnover. Magnus and Evelyn had watched at least a hundred employees come and go over the years.

"She's a nice one," Archie said, gathering up his plate, silverware and glass. "Hilary, that was magnificent. I won't be telling my mum how good your bread is."

"Charming," the older woman said, with a shake of her head. She was only about fifteen years older than Archie but there was something very serious and reserved by the way she carried herself around the house. He knew her late husband had been in the military and their only son lived in Japan, but Hilary didn't seem interested in sharing too many details of her life. "And there's chocolate cake on the counter."

"Oh no, more secrets to keep," Archie teased. "Do you mind if I take it down to the pool house? I have some reading to do."

"Go right ahead. Coffee's not ready yet though."

"I'll bring him down some later," Magnus cut in. "During my evening walk."

"You're both spoiling me tonight. Can't say that I mind." Archie brought everything over to the sink, rinsing in the double sink before loading it into the industrial dishwasher. He looked out the window onto the back patio, barely able to make out the in-ground pool and beyond it, the small stone house that served as his room when he stayed over on the estate. A perk, as it were. His old room was now part of Hilary's apartments and God forbid his majesty give Archie one of the ten guest rooms peppering the first and second floors.

"Hilary?" Henry's voice jolted him. Archie turned around casually as he put his glass into the dishwasher's top rack.

"Henry—here for some food?" Hilary asked, quickly getting off the stool to greet her employer's son.

"Please, don't get up. If you could just point out the plate." Henry wasn't looking at Archie, not directly. "I don't want to disturb your dinner."

"It's right here, no problem at all." Hilary hurried to one of the three microwaves on the counter, opening the middle one. "Do you need something to drink?"

"I'll grab a soda from the refrigerator, thank you." Henry walked around the large island in the center of the room, to the double-door fridge, one of two in the expansive space. Archie could see Henry's gaze falling to where he stood.

"Nice and warm." Hilary waited in the center of the kitchen, clearly unsure of where to put the plate.

Archie closed the dishwasher then wiped his hand on a dishtowel.

"I'll take that." Henry crossed the room, hands out to take the plate from the housekeeper, smiling the entire time. "Do you mind if I eat in here?"

"Oh, of course not."

Magnus got out of his chair, pulling on his jacket at the same time. "You can have my seat sir. I'm off to close to house for the night."

"Thank you." Henry gave a quick look over his shoulder to Archie who was busying himself at the cake plate, cutting himself a large slice.

It felt silly, the act and routine of them pretending to be employer/employee in front of Magnus. Even if Archie never acted like Henry was his lover, at least he could let down his guard. Show they were friends, acknowledge they had grown up together. But that wasn't the script—the day Archie became an employee, everything changed. Everyone in this house was so locked into their roles, no one verbalizing any objections, with Henry being the number one offender. Archie wanted to shake it up: throw a dish, curse out loud, storm into the dining room and tell Norman to unclench for five fucking minutes.

But he didn't.

"Good night then," he said finally as he took a fork from the silverware drawer.

Henry and Hilary murmured good nights to him from the table, Magnus raised his hand.

"Coffee later," he called and Archie gave him a big smile.

"Lovely."

He and his cake headed to the back door; he slipped out quickly and quietly, eager to be in the cool autumn night air and not in the fakery of the kitchen. And his own complicity.

THERE WAS no way around it—Henry was in full sneaking mode.

Down the center staircase of his father's home at half past midnight, shoes in hand, like a wayward teenager trying to avoid detection. Never had he been more grateful for Norman's rooms being in their own wing, so far from his. Never had he been more grateful his father and stepmother went to bed religiously at ten, meaning they were very much asleep and highly unlikely to find him creeping past the entryway and through the kitchen to the back door.

Faintly horrifying and undignified, that's what it was.

Henry pushed down the need to turn around—because the only thing worse than having to sneak around your childhood home as an adult man was reprimanding yourself into going back to bed. He shoved the need to follow the rules—his father's rules—deep down as he disabled the back-door alarm, then slipped outside into the night.

The sweater he'd pulled on had been a good idea, a clear score in the column of "overly conscientious," as the sunny May day had turned chilly after sunset. He paused to slip on his loafers, tucking himself beside the door, between two large pots of herbs.

Without the patio lights on, it was pitch-black between the back door and the gate in the wall surrounding the pool area, but this was

Henry's childhood home and he could navigate it without a stumble. In the distance he could see the pool house's lights, which meant he was officially out of reasons not to move.

Quietly he darted around the boxwood hedges and down the precisely placed pavers. Henry reached the gate and slowly pulled it open, hands jittering on the old brass lock. No one from the house could hear him this far away, but he also thought it a bad idea to draw Archie out of the pool house, armed and ready for intruders.

Henry wasn't an intruder; he was just a sneak.

The in-ground pool sat silent, still under the protection of its winter cover. All the lounge chairs and tables were tucked away in the storage unit, spending the cold months out of sight until they were required for summer events.

As Henry reached the pool house, a sizable structure that would probably go for six figures in the right tony neighborhood, he paused. Nervous tension welled up inside his stomach, the hesitation that had prevented a thousand roads taken in his life. Knocking on that door meant a confrontation, a conversation he was dreading.

The safer, smarter thing would be to return to the house and pretend nothing was wrong.

But Henry was a coward, not stupid. He shook his head, swallowing hard as he took the last few steps to the red-painted door of the stone house. His knock was firm, decisive.

Also a lie.

"Coming." Archie's voice was muffled through the door.

The door opened, and Archie looked through the sliver of space. He'd changed out of his suit into sweatpants and a Gold's Gym T-shirt, left behind from a previous visit; the bare feet and wire-rimmed glasses made Henry smile just a little bit.

This man was gorgeous.

"Hi." Archie's expression and voice were cool, but he pulled the door wider so Henry could come in. "It's late."

"Am I disturbing you?" Henry brushed his shoulder against Archie's.

"No, no. Just finished my reading, actually."

The small stone house was decorated with things left over after the various redesign whims of the multiple Mrs. Walkers. That meant a hodgepodge of couches, tables, and artwork ranging in style from early Americana to French country to Louis XIV. It looked like a very expensive yard sale gone horribly wrong.

Archie had a few lamps lit around the square created from four large sofas, each a totally different style. A low wooden chest—from an ill-advised West Indies phase of his second stepmother's—sat in the center, Archie's place held in his novel with the television remote. A collection of mismatched pillows was stacked at one end of the largest couch, a heavy cable-stitch throw casually tossed aside. Archie's study nest, cozy and warm.

"I would've brought you a cup of coffee…." Henry started to say, speaking to Archie's back as he walked over to his comfy perch.

"Magnus stopped by with some." Archie gestured toward a delicate Queen Anne end table tucked between the sofas, taking a tall silver thermos in his hands. "The butler delivering me my coffee—Mum would be tickled by the sight," he teased.

"Oh." Henry stared at the floor, suddenly filled with the recollection of his eighteenth birthday and this pool house and Archie and the stolen bottle of $800 champagne that had started them down this terribly confusing—wonderful—road.

Archie sprawled on the couch, pulling his legs up. He fussed with the thermos, pouring himself some coffee into the metal cup. "Sit down, you're making me nervous."

"Right." Awkwardness permeated the room, but Henry wasn't ready to give up and return to the house. He really did mean to smooth over—at least some things.

"Did you want some wine?" Archie's gaze flickered to Henry.

Henry shook his head, hands fluttering a bit at his side as he tried to decide what to do. He needed to choose between where Archie was and a seat farther away. "Not right now."

He picked the couch Archie was on.

Archie's eyebrows rose, but he didn't say anything.

They sat in pregnant silence, broken only by the distant rattle of wind against the gate beyond the little house.

"You should take a day off next week to make it up to Evelyn. I'm sure she was disappointed you missed dinner," Henry said finally.

Archie was already shaking his head.

"She understands. More than anyone, really." His mother had clocked over twenty-five years as the Walker housekeeper, and only the stroke last year had slowed down her devotion to the family.

Henry toyed with the hem of his sweater to give his hands something to do. "That's fine. But I insist, okay? You need a day off."

"Yes. Sir." Archie adopted a lower register, complete with proper British accent.

"Idiot," Henry said fondly. "You sound like Norman."

Archie made a sound of derision, then immediately took a sip of coffee.

"What?"

"Nothing."

"What?" Henry asked again. They'd known each other since they were barely out of diapers. "Nothing" didn't cut it.

Archie gestured expansively, leaning his head back against the pillows. "It's so… ridiculous up here. So fake. *Downton Abbey* bullshit. Sometimes I go through the motions for hours before I realize how stupid it is. Like driving an hour and a half for no reason."

"He asked to have dinner with me," Henry interrupted and almost instantly wanted to take it back. Because it was ridiculous and inconsiderate and exactly the sort of thing his father did on a regular basis. If he truly wanted dinner with his only son, he could have had it in Manhattan, after work. Not upstate, not in the middle of the week, and the night before a big meeting.

Not when the invitation sounded much more like a summoning. Not when it disrupted Henry's life and, by extension, Archie's.

Of course he didn't say that.

"Right, but—" Archie cut himself off with the cup to his lips, his eyes a sea storm of frustration.

"I know. And I'm sorry to drag you away from your studies and your evening with your mother. I'm just not good at saying no to him."

Understatement of the century, punctuated by the upward quirk of Archie's left eyebrow.

Henry shifted in the soft cushions of the couch. It felt disloyal to complain about his father; he wasn't very good at it, even when he agreed with what people were saying.

"Sorry," Archie said with a sigh, leaning over to put the metal cup on the table. "I'm just tired, and I have a lot on my mind, with graduation coming up."

The silence descended again. Henry's brain ticked through so many things he got a tiny bit dizzy; he closed his eyes against the memories and the worries and the deal they were closing tomorrow with Breen Steel.

And the thing he'd come here in the first place to say.

"I'm sorry for the thing in the car," Henry said finally, when he was done feeling like a ridiculous coward and aware—particularly tonight, particularly after the conversation with his father before dinner—of how little time he and Archie might have together.

Literally and metaphorically.

Archie was already shaking his head.

"No, no. I overreacted."

Archie's good-natured smile faltered a little. He looked away, blue eyes fixated on the Shaker-style bookshelf in the corner. It held assorted Buddha statues and ships in bottles.

"I want to be done with school." Archie directed his gaze back to Henry. "I'm proud of my grades, proud to be graduating in a few weeks—even if it did take me twice as long."

The *as you* hung in the air. When they were kids, it had been easier to pretend things weren't so different. This wasn't a staged period piece. The boss's son, the housekeeper's kid, playing and being best friends—that was natural.

Until you grew up and there were things like expectations and debts and responsibilities and two very different paths in life.

"I'm so proud of you," Henry murmured. "I know you'll be successful at whatever you choose to do."

Archie didn't respond, but his gaze was locked on Henry's face; it burned and left Henry a bit short of breath.

"I don't know about that," he said finally. "Bodyguard and chauffeur are hardly proof I know anything in regard to international business relations," he said lightly, rubbing his palms against his thighs as he finally looked away. "Could probably use a recommendation from Mr. Norman Henry Walker III."

"You know I'll do anything I can," Henry said, his voice gentle. He resisted the urge to reach out and touch Archie's socked foot, so close to his own leg.

"Trying to get rid of me, eh?"

The joke was well-intentioned, Henry knew, but after his father's pontification on Archie moving to greener pastures earlier in the evening—well, it stung, and Henry felt himself stiffening into ramrod straightness.

"Yes. I can't imagine who we'll be able to find to open my door and drive the Hummer." Henry fell into lofty pronouncements, tossing his head to punctuate the words. It only served to knock a hank of heavy blond hair into his eyes.

"Or fuck you senseless three nights a month," Archie lobbed back, and Henry's eyes narrowed.

"That won't be a requirement of your replacement."

Archie regarded him over the small ovals of his lenses. A thousand unspoken words seem to bounce between them—an easy communication borne of being together almost every day of their childhoods and so many days beyond that.

"Good to know," Archie drawled, poking his feet into Henry's thigh.

Neither of them mentioned the giant elephant in the room, which was calmly sitting in the corner on a colonial wingback next to a Tiffany floor lamp. What would happen when Archie graduated and moved on?

Secret rendezvous didn't spontaneously happen when you had to pick up the phone and admit you were involved.

"Don't let your ego go crazy." Henry rested his hand on Archie's ankle, absently pushing Archie's sweats up to get to his lover's perpetually warm flesh. "I'm not saying you're… irreplaceable or anything."

"Mmmm." Archie's voice softened as he took his glasses off and folded them, laying them near his book. He sat up, switching his position so now he was leaning against Henry's side, hip to hip. Henry welcomed the way Archie's big, broad body shifted closer to him. If they couldn't use their words to communicate like big boys, they could always use their bodies to fill the silence.

"You smell so good," Archie whispered as he kissed behind Henry's ear, nosing the blond hair out of the way. Their painful attempts at adult conversation usually ended like this, and Archie was starting to be concerned that he'd developed a Pavlovian response to their awkward talks—he got horny. He shifted to lean over Henry's toned and lean body, resting his hand on the cushion. Slowly he made his way down Henry's throat, licking at his pulse, then sucking gently.

Henry moved restlessly under Archie's hands; Archie knew when he wanted to be held down, knew when he liked it fast and rough.

"Take off your clothes," Archie murmured when his mouth hit material. He lifted his head, inches away from Henry's lips now.

Henry's dark blue eyes flashed hotly. A glimpse of pink tongue tantalized Archie as Henry licked at his lips.

"Make me."

It wasn't a question; it was barely a request. Just a soft crackle of words—more a whisper.

The couch creaked this time when Archie moved, and he sighed with annoyance. This was much easier in Henry's enormous bed back in Manhattan.

"Let's go to the bedroom, then." Archie kissed the side of Henry's mouth, marveled at his soft lips, and then the masculine curve of his jaw. Whatever collection of genes, magic, and chance had put Henry together, Archie was forever in their debt.

It was a scramble then, getting up and moving with lustful intentions and painful hard-ons. Archie followed Henry into the small second room of the pool house—a tiny bedroom that barely had enough oxygen for the two of them and a sleigh bed jammed under the windows.

Archie had one arm looped around Henry's chest, keeping him close—he snapped the switch with his free hand, throwing weak patterns of light from the sconces on the wall. Archie ground against Henry, enjoying his frustrated mutterings as he pushed back eagerly.

"We're here—now get on with it." Henry twisted his neck, biting at Archie's jaw.

Archie let Henry go, giving him a good slap on the ass. "Bitchy."

Henry didn't respond, just gave him a glare over his shoulder before kicking off his loafers. He gave Archie a brief show—the arch of his back, the line of his broad shoulders tapering into a narrow waist as he yanked off the sweater he was wearing and threw it to the floor. Archie palmed himself, gaze following every flex of muscles under Henry's T-shirt.

"That it?"

"I believe I told you to make me," Henry said, turning around to face Archie. One hip crooked to the side—a coquettish pose Archie knew well.

All the tension of the day—the last-minute summoning to the estate, the fight packed with subtext, the lack of resolution—bloomed into something red-hot under Archie's skin. He loved to fuck Henry—loved it. But sometimes it went beyond that, to something primal.

"Come here, brat," he teased, if only to see Henry roll his eyes.

"No."

"Take off your clothes."

Henry looked at the ceiling, his expression bemused. "No."

Archie stalked over to him, using his height advantage to cast a long shadow over his lover. He reached out, and when Henry dodged him, he growled.

There wasn't anywhere to go. The wall was inches behind Henry, the bed a foot to their left. Henry didn't flinch when Archie grabbed the fabric of his T-shirt, yanked him closer.

Didn't even blink.

And maybe that was their problem, at the end of the day.

Their bodies twined dangerously close, their mouths hovering near a kiss—but that didn't happen; it rarely happened. Archie didn't think too much about it as he pulled the shirt over Henry's head.

"Is there…."

"My back pocket," Henry whispered, breathless now as Archie reached for Henry's fly.

"Slut."

Henry laughed, then licked his lips slowly. As Archie undid Henry's button, then zipper, the other man's gaze was locked on Archie's tented sweatpants.

Archie maneuvered him onto the bed, guiding with rough hands until Henry was laid out across the navy-blue duvet. He threw the pillows on the floor, then followed them with his T-shirt and sweats, stripping with military efficiency.

Henry watched him from the bed, khakis undone and bare-chested, beautiful, and breathless.

With eager motions Archie pulled the pants off Henry's body, revealing the entirety of his golden skin and strong, masculine lines.

"Back pocket?"

"Mmmm."

Archie rifled through the pocket and pulled out a condom, a small package of lube, and a wet wipe.

Archie groaned as Henry snickered, laying his forearm over his eyes.

"What? I'm prepared."

"You're the sluttiest of all Eagle Scouts, Henry, now and forever."

"You say the sweetest things, and you're still going to fuck me, right?"

He didn't bother to answer because it was a given—Henry hadn't sneaked into the pool house to chat or resolve their fight. He'd come down here to get fucked, and Archie meant to oblige.

Archie threw everything onto the bed. He crawled over Henry's body, feeling warm skin against his own. He mapped Henry's chest with lips and tongue, pausing to suck his nipples and flick the nubs lightly.

"Henry," he murmured, slipping lower, nipping at his navel. He could feel the blunt head of Henry's cock against his chin and groaned, biting off the wave of need that slammed him down hard, leaving him panting against Henry's skin.

Henry moved restlessly against him, gripping one hand in the covers, the other against Archie's shoulder. He held him and pushed him at the same time—that urging for him to hurry the hell up.

Sliding his tongue over Henry's cock, Archie drew it into his mouth, licking at the head, tracing his tongue slowly along the slit. The salty fluid there left Archie groaning as he dropped his mouth all the way to the base of Henry's dick.

Moaning and breathless sounds filled his ears, the pounding of his heartbeat a bass line underneath Henry's needy whispers. He sucked slowly, the length of Henry's cock lying against his tongue and pressing against the back of his throat.

It was amazingly good and not nearly enough. Archie felt desire jackhammering at his brain as he reached for the lube, feeling around for it among the folds of the coverlet. He pulled off with a dirty, sucking pop, licking his lips as his gaze found Henry's face.

There weren't words for this—it just happened, a near perfect repeat of their first time. No champagne, though, no long-held crushes coming to fruition in this very room. Just sex—their version of conversation.

Henry moved then, as if reading Archie's thoughts. He pulled his legs up and shifted, rolling over to hands and knees.

Archie's brain melted another tick, his hands moving of their own accord to open the lube container.

It was mechanics then, their routine of touch and sounds and Henry coming undone under Archie's rough fingers. Stoic Henry, proper Henry, Henry in a three-piece suit—Henry begging and whining for Archie to "hurry up and fuck me."

"Yes, sir," Archie teased, all faux British and a tight grip on Henry's hips.

Eyes closing, Archie pressed forward, shuddering as Henry's body yielded around him, tight like a glove. When he was as deep as he could go, Archie paused and looked down at the beautiful line of Henry's back. "Fucking perfect."

He moved his hips, rocking him into Henry over and over, faster, deeper. Archie shuddered, his entire body tense as he held back long enough to wrap one hand around Henry's cock, stroking with that same relentless rhythm.

"So good, fuck, take it." Nonsense poured out of Archie's mouth, dirty talk and bitten-off curses. He could feel sweat forming on his skin, the point of contact where his and Henry's bodies met molten hot. The bed creaked loudly, the frame knocking against the wall.

He moved his fist over Henry's cock in the exact way Archie knew would drag his orgasm from him. He dropped his mouth to the center of his lover's back, licking and biting where he knew it wouldn't be seen.

Henry didn't say a word, absorbed every stroke and slam of Archie's body in near silence. It drove Archie mad when he was quiet. It made him move faster and harder until everything blurred into frantic, angry movement.

Archie held off long enough to feel Henry's body stiffen, to feel the spill of wetness against his palm as his lover came. He let the twitches and shudders coax him into letting go, pulsing into the condom.

The sudden silence was almost deafening. Archie pressed his lips to Henry's shoulder, his version of a kiss, and began to marshal his muscles into working again. He pulled out, his one clean hand steady against Henry's spine, murmuring comforting sounds as Henry twitched.

Hard and fast always came back to haunt you.

"Something to drink?" Archie's voice was a rasp. He got off the bed carefully, watching Henry as he rolled to his side with a sigh.

"Yeah. The wine?" Henry didn't look at him, just tucked into a ball with his face hidden by his forearm.

"Right."

Archie went into the tiny bathroom, narrowly missing a bash to the head by an awkwardly hung shelf. He washed up, then hid the used condom deep in a pile of tissues at the bottom of the wastebasket. Hilary would be tidying up after he left in the morning, and there was nothing about her finding a condom that he wanted to deal with.

Technically he was on duty.

Technically he'd just fucked his boss.

After the bathroom he headed for the wine refrigerator tucked into the corner of the main room. Archie checked the front door—it was double locked—and then made a quick pass of the windows. He shut off the lights and reset the alarm before making his way back to the bedroom, wine in one hand and two juice glasses in the other.

"Henry?" he called out as a courtesy and was rewarded with a sleepy grunt.

Henry was under the covers, back to the wall. The bed wasn't conducive to two grown men, both over six feet—Archie significantly so—sleeping comfortably, but Henry clearly wasn't leaving for a while.

Archie—hiding his pleasure at this—poured them each a healthy portion of the wine, using the narrow dresser as his bar.

"Not too much. I have that meeting tomorrow."

"Right, I remember," Archie said drily. "I have that meeting too—at least the transportation part."

Henry came out from under the covers—just his head though. The messy hair elicited a snicker from Archie.

"What?"

"I'm setting the alarm for five. You need to do something about that just-fucked hairdo." Archie sat down on the bed. He offered a glass to Henry, who was scowling.

"So helpful."

"I live to serve, my liege."

Archie settled against the headboard; they shared a quick clink of glasses, falling into a comfortable silence.

Chapter Three

Archie woke up at five to the angry trill of his phone alarm; he groaned as he sat up, trying to orient himself without rolling off the bed. Vaguely, he remembered Henry disentangling himself from the heap of limbs in which they'd fallen asleep and heading back to the house. He remembered finishing the last glass of wine, then going back to sleep afterward.

That had clearly been a mistake.

The wine hangover followed him from the bed to the tiny shower in the bathroom. Archie leaned against the wall until the cold water woke him up enough to open his eyes the whole way.

Huge miscalculation. He could have probably drained every water tank at the estate and still not shocked his body into wakefulness.

Archie was pissed now—he didn't like appearing unprofessional, and he hated having his body out of his control, and this morning he was borderline on both.

And of course this was the morning he'd have a bad reaction to wine. When he had to drive all the way back to the city with Mr. Walker in the car, with Henry being tense and strained sitting back there alongside David Silver, the senior vice president and Norman's right hand. It was a combination Archie hated to witness.

While he toweled off, he checked his reflection and decided to chance not shaving. Everything after that was quick and routine, or as quick and routine as he could get feeling like his stomach was filled with angry, oily bees—brush his teeth, apply deodorant, get into his spare uniform, clean any lint off the impeccable black suit, put on his shoes, strap on his gun holster. He took a second to tidy up the bathroom so Hilary didn't have to do it, and then hurried to grab his already packed bag, tucking his book and reading glasses in a side pocket.

He needed to have the car in front of the house by six fifteen, and being late was never an option.

After all that rushing, Archie was only about two minutes behind schedule, nothing to panic about, but he could feel his palms sweating as he pulled the vehicle in front of the house. Norman was already on the stairs, checking his watch with a faint frown. Stomach in knots, Archie left the vehicle idling, then hopped out, a serious expression locked on to his face.

"Sir," he murmured, coming up the stairs.

"Archie."

"May I take your briefcase?"

"What? No, that's all right." Norman looked up from his watch and gave Archie a penetrating stare, which somehow managed to level up Archie's hangover. "We're waiting for Henry. He's late," Norman said, his voice tight. Norman didn't handle delays well.

"Yes, sir," Archie replied. He glanced at the door, willing his lover to hurry the hell up. The sun seemed to be beating down on his head with vindictive force.

He reached into his pocket for his aviators. Once they were slipped on, the morning got a bit easier. Archie breathed through his nose, shifting his posture so his spine was aligned over his hips, arms at his sides.

From this vantage point he could sneak glances at his employer, watching him frown and huff.

The resemblance between Henry and Norman was hard to see. Occasionally there would be a certain tilt to their heads that made it clearer; sometimes it was in the way they got annoyed at silly little things or disappeared into stony silence when something went wrong. It was found in tiny quirks, like an abhorrence of pepper and a love of sweet tea.

But Henry looked like his late mother, which no one mentioned but everyone knew.

They stood awkwardly, Archie on the bottom step of the estate's grand stairs, Norman a few steps up, still occasionally glancing at his watch with an irritated twitch, then suddenly glancing at Archie with an intensity of interest he'd never really shown—not in twenty-plus years and certainly not recently. Sweat began to collect at the back of Archie's neck.

"You're graduating soon, then?" he asked suddenly, his posh British accent cutting through the cool morning air.

The Heir Apparent

Archie tried not to jump five feet off the ground.

"Yes, sir. Six weeks."

"Hmmm." Norman didn't elaborate. "Henry will be available for recommendations should the need arise."

Archie blinked.

"Yes, sir. Thank you. That's very kind."

"My assistant, Maria, can also be of help with expediting human resources issues. You can contact her directly."

Archie forced a smile. "I appreciate that, sir."

"Have you begun looking for a position?"

"Yes, sir."

"Anything substantial?"

Archie's stomach did a double back flip loop. He licked his lips subtly. "Ferelli and Sons—I have a third interview tomorrow."

Norman fixed his steely gaze on Archie for a full—painful, terrible—minute.

"They're an excellent firm. You would do good work there. Please tell Edgar I send my best."

Archie almost swallowed his tongue.

"Thank you, sir."

"Mmmm." Norman checked his watch again, huffed an impatient sigh. "How is your mother then?"

"Very well, thank you."

"Please give her our regards."

"Of course."

The pulsing storm of his headache upgraded to a typhoon behind his eyes. He tried to remember if there was aspirin in the bag of supplies he kept under his seat.

And maybe he was hallucinating the most personal conversation he'd had with Norman Walker since he was seventeen years old and had become a full-time employee. Say hello to Edgar Ferelli? Was that as good as a recommendation or two?

"Norman, darling? Are you sure you don't want tea?"

The current Mrs. Walker exited the huge double doors of the massive Tudor, already dressed for the day in a green twinset and modest black skirt. With her Bettie Page hairstyle and fifties-era shoes, she looked like a classic gangster-movie heroine.

Norman sighed. "No, Libby, it's fine. I'll have something at the meeting." He finally looked up, leaning in to kiss his wife as she came to stand next to him.

"Good morning, Archie."

"Ma'am."

Libby Walker was only a few years older than Archie but possibly the nicest in Henry's endless parade of stepmothers. At least this one had no interest in mothering him. Or ignoring him. Or hating him.

"Did you sleep well?" she asked politely.

"Yes, ma'am. Thank you." Archie fidgeted slightly. Everyone was being so damned friendly today, and it was starting to creep him out.

"Please give your mother our regards when you see her."

"I will."

And yes, he remembered, aspirin was just a few feet away. And a bottle of water, thank God. Once he'd deposited the Walkers and their senior vice president at the meeting, he was going to find a quiet spot and sleep this shitty reaction off before he ultimately had to face his mother for lunch.

The door opened again, and Henry emerged, his face white and his expression flustered as he jogged down the steps.

"My apologies," he said, slightly out of breath. "I overslept."

"Clearly." Norman kissed Libby chastely on the cheek. "Goodbye, darling. I should be home by five."

"I'll have tea waiting," Libby said cheerfully. She gave Henry a pat on the arm as he passed by. "Good luck at your meeting."

"Thank you, Libby." Henry bounced on the step, waiting for his father to walk ahead to the Hummer first.

Archie and Libby exchanged pleasant smiles, and he moved a second ahead of Norman. He reached the door and waited, poised to open it.

All part of the routine. All part of the show.

He and Henry shared a quick glance, but then it was all business and moving and arranging the crease of one's pants to avoid wrinkles.

They were on the road a few minutes later, Norman clearly opting for silent disapproval over a reprimand. By the time they pulled in front of David Silver's impressive estate fifteen minutes away, the heavy air in the Hummer was nearly visible.

Archie jumped out of the vehicle and opened the back door. David Silver exited the front door of the house a second later, smiling benignly at him as if trying to remember his name.

"Archie." He didn't wait for a reply, just climbed into the back of the Hummer and waited for Archie to shut the door.

More bullshit. More show.

They were off again a few minutes later, speeding toward Westchester. Archie took back roads, trying to avoid the Thruway until the last possible second. Traffic made Norman tense, and Archie's main directive this morning was to keep that from happening.

The headache and nausea continued to plague him, not enough to affect his driving but still persistent and irritating. He sped down the rural roads, past horse farms and mansions, his thoughts on getting his passengers to the city on time, lunch with his mother later on, seeing Henry....

Out of the corner of his eye there was a blur, heading toward the Hummer's passenger side with blinding speed. Before he could puzzle out why something was coming from the woods, the vehicle was jolted by the impact of machine against machine.

A second later he slammed forward into the steering wheel, the sound of twisting metal exploding in his head sharply. He faintly registered that the car was flying sideways, airborne, for just a second before his head connected with the driver's-side window and knocked him unconscious.

He came up for air, breaking the dark surface of consciousness with a gasp. There was so much pain coursing through his body that he wanted to wish himself back into the bliss of being out—but there were sounds beyond his gray, fuzzy vision, angry sounds. Yelling and cursing and....

Henry.

Henry shouting. Men fighting. Frantic sounds of violence just beyond his senses.

Archie rolled to his side, feeling the hard concrete of the road against his back and hip. He still couldn't see very well, and the nonspecific pain of the accident suddenly seemed to concentrate in his left thigh, which now appeared to be on fire.

Sick to his stomach, Archie forced himself onto his hand and knees; putting pressure on his left side was impossible, which led him to sit back on his heels. His head swam, more gray lines obscuring his sight.

Someone was yelling furiously in the background.

With one last force of strength, Archie struggled to stand—and almost immediately collapsed again. His left leg was useless, his sight compromised. When he reached under his jacket for his gun, his fingers met emptiness.

They had his gun.

"He's up again!" someone shouted, and Archie felt a blow slam directly between his shoulder blades. It robbed him of breath, and then once again he felt himself violently slipping away.

Chapter Four

A SOFT, foul-smelling surface cushioned the side of Henry's head; his ear pressed down, hearing muffled, a tickle of blood winding its way down his forehead like a creeping spider. Even with his eyes closed, the sensation of spinning and falling repeated over and over, until Henry could only swallow back the nausea and pray for unconsciousness again.

He could hear sounds close by—a murmur of voices with highway noise muted in the background.

"Henry?" A whispered voice came through the darkness.

He winced, ears ringing as he moved his hands weakly against slippery fabric. There was a thought to push himself up, but that, he knew, was impossible. He couldn't speak for fear of being ill, a soft breath of air escaping between his lips.

"Henry," the voice said again, shuffling closer as the surface beneath him dipped, a movement that exploded angry colors behind his eyes.

It was his father.

"Oh, son." A hand gently touched his shoulder, tentative and careful not to jostle him. "David, he's waking up," Norman said a second later, and Henry remembered that his godfather had been with them in the car.

Henry whimpered; he was not a child, not a weak man, but in that split second nothing could have made him feel better than having Norman and David there with him, both of them alive and well.

"Don't move, Henry," David said. Another hand, this time patting his wrist. "You hit your head very hard." His stern voice was calm, and Henry breathed, shivering a little against what he now realized was a mattress.

"He needs a doctor," Norman bitched, and David made a hushing noise.

"Norman, please. They can do whatever they want at this point. We just have to be cooperative and hope they contact the board with a ransom request."

"I already told them the board would pay whatever they wanted—anything, but they didn't seem interested in that." The timbre of his father's voice rose, and Henry bit his lip. His ears buzzed like he'd been hit again.

"Perhaps it's just a tactic. I wouldn't be surprised if they made us wait, then demanded we call the board ourselves for a bigger payout." David sounded disgusted.

Henry could hear David's feet scuffling along the floor as David stood, then footsteps as he moved around the space. Norman remained at Henry's side, occasionally patting his shoulder. It was the most paternal and demonstrative he could remember his father being in years.

"I'm sorry, Henry," Norman whispered suddenly, following his words with a quiet sigh. "So sorry. I would do anything to get us out of here."

Henry tried to remember anything that could connect him to this minute, anything at all. But his memories jumped around in a jumbled mix; things he thought might be from last week to this morning, to his fifth birthday. It made him wildly dizzy, so he stopped, pressing his fingers against the fabric beneath him until the looping thoughts stopped.

"Henry? Henry?" Norman's panicked whisper brought him back into awareness. He had lost consciousness, clearly, and fear began to curl up in the center of his chest.

Just how badly hurt was he?

"I'm all right, Father." Henry's voice was barely a rasp at this point. "Just a little dizzy."

"You wouldn't stop fighting them," Norman whispered. "You tried so hard."

Henry breathed deeply; it was strange to hear a story about yourself you couldn't remember.

"They hit you in the head."

It made sense, even if he couldn't connect his father's words to the incident.

"I thought...." His father's voice cracked, and Henry's chest squeezed. "I was terribly worried about you."

"Someone's coming," David said anxiously, his footsteps bringing him back over to Henry and Norman's side of the room.

The squeak and grind of a lock being turned broke the quiet, and Henry heard his father gasp. Were these the men who were refusing his father's offer of ransom? He frantically tried to open his eyes.

A door opened, then was quickly slammed shut. With fierce determination Henry cracked open his eyelids just enough to see a man's dirty work boots a few feet away.

"Here," the man rasped, throwing a heavy canvas bag close to Henry's head. It hit the side of the bed and fell to the floor, jarring the mattress, a movement that sent him back into the nauseating darkness, trying to keep his stomach from erupting.

"Can we speak to you, please?" David was saying, his voice cajoling and charming as if they were in a boardroom and not in a dire situation. "If you could just contact our offices—they will arrange to pay you whatever you want. Please. Henry needs medical attention."

"Whatever you want." That was Norman, the cool edge gone from his voice. All Henry heard was fear.

The man said nothing. The sound repeated, a door opening and closing.

They were alone.

Norman let out a few muttered curses.

"Bastard." Norman moved away, just enough, Henry estimated, to grab the bag and pull it closer. Though a fierce lion in the business community, Norman was a victim of a genetically bad heart, a fact he refused to face. But now, in their perilous situation, Henry could hear the strain in his father's breathing, the rattle in his chest.

"There's water," Norman said. "Some food. A first-aid kit, though I imagine plasters aren't going to do much good."

"Barely anything," came David's mumble. "This is disgusting."

A few seconds later Henry felt the blanket being laid over his back and shoulders.

"Where's my jacket?" he murmured, the first thing he could remember having said for ages.

"They took it. Mine too. Our shoes." Norman fussed over him; Henry felt a second blanket draped over his legs. "They're wearing masks, Henry—that man who brought the bag in, he's the only one who's spoken." His father paused. "I don't know what they want if they don't want money."

The words were dire, the sentiment edged with hopelessness. Three of the richest men in New York City, tossed into a room God knew where, at the mercy of strangers who seemingly didn't want anything.

Henry was afraid.

The fear began to spread into panic, racking his entire body.

He and his father and David had been in the Hummer, heading for a morning meeting in the city. They were discussing the Breen project when suddenly....

The accident.

But not an accident.

They had taken him from the car.

Henry's breathing sped up.

Archie.

The sickening sound of metal scraping metal. Being forced off the road, into the tree. The men who swarmed the Hummer, guns raised.

The shots they fired.

Archie.

Nothing after that, just a black hole of nothing—a jumble of voices, anger, and aggression.

But not Archie.

The fear had a companion now.

Grief.

Henry must've made a sound, because his father's hand tightened on his shoulder.

"Henry? What's wrong?"

It was force of habit to pretend when it came to Archie, pretend he was an employee, pretend he was the chauffeur, the bodyguard. Pretend they were friendly because they'd grown up together. It was a cool persona he used with his father, a tool to portray himself a certain way.

But his filter was gone, beaten out of him by silent men in masks.

"Archie," he choked out, his throat tight with pain.

"Oh." Just one flat, quiet word, and Henry's breath hitched. "It happened so quickly," his father murmured, hand flexing against Henry's arm. "He… was knocked out for a bit. Then he woke up. Tried to stop them, of course. Put up a hell of a fight."

Henry struggled to keep the tears inside, but he'd lost control of everything—his emotions, his body. All that control, knocked from him.

"He was still alive when they put us in the van," Norman said softly. "I saw him. I promise he was alive."

Norman rubbed Henry's shoulder gently, fussing with the blanket with his other hand. "Just rest, Henry. You need to lie still. We'll be fine."

Murmurs between Norman and David buzzed outside of Henry's consciousness. He alternated between silent tears and dark periods of nothing—he'd wake with a start, pain and nausea sending him back into unconsciousness almost immediately.

He lost track of time entirely.

"Henry! Henry!"

His name summoned him out of the well of bad dreams and grief—he was remembering hiding with Archie in the big oak tree at the edge of the property, eating chocolate biscuits they'd "stolen" from the kitchen. They were nine, always running around the property with dirty knees and loud shouts. Inseparable.

It was the first summer Henry realized boys could like boys the way they're supposed to like girls.

He opened his eyes with a start, feeling the urgency of hands at his shoulder.

"Henry, wake up. We heard something," his father said breathlessly as he tried to pull his son into a seated position.

"Gunshots," David added, his voice shaking.

That propelled Henry into moving even as his body and brain protested loudly.

Between his father, David, and Henry's own straining effort, they managed to get him upright and lean him against the headboard. Through blurry vision, Henry could see they were in a small, dark motel room, one window heavily blanketed with curtains. Beyond the walls Henry could hear faint popping sounds, shouts echoing outside. Norman moved in front of Henry, crouched as if shielding him from whatever was on the other side.

"Father," he whispered, but Norman shushed him.

"Stay behind me. You're in no condition to be moving around."

David vibrated with worry next to him. "Do you think it's the police?"

"Archie would have given them a description," Norman murmured. "They must've found us."

Henry could hear his father's voice lose a trace of its impeccable British tone, harkening back to its rough Dorchester roots. He also heard the labored breathing that could signal something serious.

"Father, take a breath; you have to relax," he said, touching his father's back gently.

"I'm fine, Henry."

The noise got louder, vibrations shaking the walls. Henry's chest hurt with worry and fear—he could barely move, his father had a bad heart, David was in his sixties… if things went any further south, he had no clue how they were going to survive.

Chapter Five

THE SOUNDS erupted outside the door, closer now, and Norman, still rasping and breathing heavily, closed the barely existent distance between Henry's body and his. Henry shook as he reached for his father's hand, a gesture he honestly didn't remember ever attempting.

Norman squeezed back.

The sharp sensation of fear filled the tiny space between the three men. After a ridiculously long amount of time, the door rattled, then opened.

Henry held his breath.

The barrel of an automatic weapon entered first, followed by the large, black-clothed shape of a policeman dressed in SWAT gear.

"Oh thank God," David exclaimed, scrambling to his feet with a heavy lean against the wall. "We're over here!"

The officer was already looking over, then making his way slowly over, gun still up and poised at the ready.

"Can you identify yourselves, please?" he asked, voice commanding and stern.

"Norman Walker, my son, Henry, and David Silver," Norman answered quickly. Henry hadn't let go of his hand yet. "We need an ambulance."

"Are you hurt, sir?"

"No, my son is. They struck him on the head." Norman's voice faded a bit, stumbling over the last few words.

"Father?" Henry's panic returned as his father's grip weakened.

"I'm fine."

Norman sounded anything but fine.

The officer was speaking into a radio strapped to his arm, his hushed tones urgent.

"Father, lie down, please," Henry said, urging Norman back against the headboard next to him. "Please. They're sending an ambulance; you can get checked out at the hospital."

Light flooded the room as blankets were removed. Norman's skin was pale, ashen—it was impossible to ignore that there was something terribly wrong. As he let Henry guide him back, Henry could feel the clammy dampness seeping through his father's clothing.

"I'm...." Norman's efforts to insist he was fine fell into a heavy sigh.

"Good God, tell the paramedics to hurry," David told the policeman. "He has a bad heart."

No, Henry wanted to point out. His father had a barely working heart. Despite the best in medical care, Norman had a cardio system hampered by poor genetics, lack of personal care, and battered by two heart attacks. Both attacks had happened while Henry was away from home—once at college, the other on a business trip—but he'd had the symptoms to watch for drilled into his head by his father's doctor, and most recently, Libby.

All those things were happening now.

"Mr. Walker?" The second man knelt beside Norman, flicking his gaze to Henry. He reached down to take Norman's pulse, turning again to the standing officer when he got no response from Norman.

"Hayes, find out where the paramedics are." The man's tone never changed, but Henry's terror ratcheted up.

"Father? Father?" Henry pulled his father closer to him, trying to get a response, to feel him breathing at the very least.

"Hayes?"

"They're down the hall, coming up."

The voices swarmed around Henry, but his attention was entirely focused on Norman, who had somehow shrunk from the larger-than-life man Henry had always perceived him to be. He felt tiny in Henry's arms. Frail.

"Father?"

"Hen...." It was a whisper, but Norman responded. Henry blinked frantically, trying to clear his vision.

Norman tried again to say Henry's name, but he didn't get past the first syllable.

"Don't talk. The paramedics are coming." He drew their faces close, nearly forehead to forehead so he could see. "It's all right."

"S... ssss...." Norman's breathing was growing more and more labored. It was rasps now; Henry could feel the physical difficulty his father was having against his own chest.

"It's all right, Father. Relax."

Shouting, sounds of clattering erupted into the room. Henry tightened his grip on Norman's shaking form.

Norman struggled weakly, but he was trying to move, trying to sit up—something. Henry couldn't be sure, but he held on, as if sheer will could propel his father's heart to continue to work.

Someone tried to pull him away, and it shouldn't have taken much—he was weak and dizzy—but he wouldn't let go.

"You can stay close, but let us work, please," a woman's voice said, and Henry nodded, releasing his father into the hands of the two paramedics who had arrived, trailing equipment and more policemen.

They moved Norman to the floor of the motel room, lights flipping on and more people milling about. They stripped open his shirt, one taking vitals while the other listened to his breathing with a stethoscope.

Henry's gaze clouded over with tears and dizziness. He pressed against the wall in an attempt to steady himself, to keep from falling apart. How had this day gone like this? Who had those people been?

"Sir? Mr. Walker?"

Henry turned his head to find a dark-haired man in a suit squatting down to his level.

"I'm Agent Feller with the FBI. I need to speak with you."

Henry shook his head, turning back to his father's still form, watching as the paramedics' movements grew more and more frantic. His own heart squeezed with fear.

"Mr. Walker, I'm sorry, but we have to talk."

The loud beep of a portable heart monitor pierced the air. It was then the only thing Henry heard, the audible evidence his father was still alive.

A hand touched his arm, but he shook it off. A stretcher appeared, another paramedic, more police officers in the room, but Henry listened to the monitor.

The sound changed pitch. Dropped off, then returned with earsplitting terror.

A switch flipped. Henry could only stare in dazed horror as the paramedics began to frantically try to revive his father there on the ground. Their movements were a blur, their complicated medical conversation washing over him like an ocean wave. He struggled to stay on his feet, to keep his eyes open because no—no. This couldn't be happening.

How could this be happening?

"I have a heartbeat," someone said, and the forward motion began once again. Norman's body—ripped-open clothes, attached to wires, and covered with the hands of the people trying to save him—was placed on the stretcher. And then they were gone, racing to the ambulance.

"Have to go with him," he whispered, not knowing if anyone was close enough to hear.

"You need to be checked out," a voice said, and Henry turned in the direction of the sound.

"Agent Feller," the man repeated, grasping Henry's forearm. "Let's get you to the hospital."

He tried to resist, tried to get them to put him in the ambulance with his father, but to no avail. By the time he stumbled into the sunlight, the sirens were screaming in the distance, and fresh-faced, calm paramedics were walking toward him through a crowded parking lot filled with sirens, lights, and a swarm of uniforms.

They asked questions about the date and time, who he was and where he lived. Henry didn't care.

"My father," he repeated over and over, numb with shock and terror. "Please."

Eventually they laid him on the stretcher; the FBI agent climbed in to sit near the door, his gaze never leaving Henry's face.

Henry closed his eyes, swallowing back tears.

When he opened them again, he was moving. He watched the blue sky turn into a ceiling, and then turn into a path of frosted-glass lights over his head. Murmurs and introductions, more doctors and nurses. Henry saw just a hazy blur.

Was this shock? Was his brain injured?

Where was his father?

And Archie....

He tamped down on that immediately. He had to take what David had said to heart—Archie must be alive. Must be. How else would the police have found them so quickly?

"Mr. Walker?" A new voice caught his attention. "My name is Dr. Brighton."

"My father." Henry turned his head with effort, fixing the young man with his gaze. "Please tell me where he is. I have to see him."

The expression on the doctor's face caved Henry's chest in with grief.

"Mr. Walker, they're working on him right now. As soon as I hear...."

"He's dead, isn't he?" The words spilled from Henry's lips, the sound high and shaky. "He's dead."

"They're doing everything they can," the man murmured, and Henry nodded, eyes snapping shut.

TIME PASSED in the cubicle: Dr. Brighton with his little white light, a tech who took far too much blood, another who stripped Henry out of his clothes—which then disappeared into a large brown bag—and helped him into a gown. Henry didn't speak, didn't respond. He just wanted to pretend this was a terrible dream for a while longer.

Agent Feller finally returned, black-suited and grim. Dr. Brighton hovered at his side.

"Mr. Walker, I'm sorry to have to tell you this."

The rest was just the noise of bees, furiously swarming his head until he blacked out.

HENRY WOKE up to find himself in yet another room, this one private with dimmed lighting and the faint hum of machinery. He blinked through the haze of medication and confusion, the swarm in his head still angrily filling the space between his ears. It took a few rounds of think-pause-think for everything to return to him.

He was in the hospital with a severe concussion.

He was in the hospital because he and his father and David had been kidnapped.

His father was dead.

The grief tightened his throat and chest with its viselike grip; he closed his eyes against the tears, body shaking with the effort not to yell at the top of his lungs.

Henry gripped the blanket weakly. He felt the hard plastic of the Call button under his fingers and pressed once, unsure of what he needed precisely but desperate for information.

He wanted to know where Libby was. He wanted to know if David was all right. He wanted to know if someone had called Archie's mother and his heart seized up as if the heart attack that had killed his father was now coming for him.

Archie. He needed to know Archie was all right.

He couldn't bear this; he just couldn't. The panic roared, blew in out of nowhere, squeezing his lungs and not letting a single drop of air back in. His father and Archie, the two people he loved, the constants in his life, and he had failed them both. Failed to protect them, failed to utter the words he felt in his heart, failed to be the man they both insisted he was….

"Sir? Sir—you need to focus on my voice. Mr. Walker? Come on, deep breath."

A woman's voice murmured from above him; he realized he had closed his eyes and now couldn't open them. Breathing was her request—and that was impossible at this moment.

"Mr. Walker, I'm giving you something in your IV. It's going to help. But I need you to try and take a breath." Hands touched his wrist, his forearm. The IV tube tugged slightly against the curve of his inner arm. "Come on, Mr. Walker. One breath."

It broke out of him like a sob, a giant gulp of air as he wheezed painfully. Spots of random light exploded behind his eyes, and the pain that had been simmering in his skull since the men had hit him spun almost out of control.

But he was breathing. And the woman's voice seemed pleased.

"There you go. Keep going; you're just having a panic attack."

Just… just a panic attack. Just dying, like everyone else today.

Whatever she put into the IV—along with his own labored breaths—eased his pain a bit. His eyelids fluttered, then opened, and he looked at the hazy outline of his caregiver.

She reminded him of his assistant, Kit, or rather what Kit would look like in twenty years; competent and kind.

"Better?"

Henry nodded, tiny, painful movements against the pillow.

"Understandable with all you've gone through." She patted his wrist. "I have some people anxious to see you, but if you're not feeling up to it, you can say no."

"Wh-who?" he asked, lips and mouth dry.

"Mrs. Walker?" The hesitation of her tone alluded to her not knowing Libby's relationship to him. "And an FBI agent."

Henry's head spun, and he blinked up at the nurse. Tears pooled in the corners of his eyes.

"I'll tell them to wait for a while."

"No, no. Please." Henry licked his lips weakly. "Please. Mrs. Walker—Libby. I need to speak to her."

"Okay. But as soon as you need them to go, I'll clear the room. Deal?"

Henry nodded again, and the nurse stepped away from his bedside. He heard the faint whisper of the door, then a murmur of voices from beyond it.

Libby. He'd let her down, and she was going to hate him for it, like he hated himself.

The door opened again, and Henry's eyes closed without his permission. He waited for the screams, the angry words. So he was unprepared for the muffled whisper of his name and the tight clasp of another hand in his.

"Henry."

He opened his eyes to find a haggard-looking Libby leaning over him, eyes red and hair a mess. He could hardly bear to look at her, to see the naked pain on her face.

"I'm sorry," he whispered, but Libby shook her head violently.

"Stop. I'm just so glad you're all right," she murmured, choking back a punctuating sob. "We couldn't bear to lose you too." Her voice broke, and she dropped her head to his shoulder as her entire body shook.

His arms felt like they were made of lead, but Henry managed to get his left hand high enough to pat her shoulder. He could feel her tears seeping through his hospital gown and into his skin, winding their way into his heart.

"I'm sorry," he said again, letting her grieve, feeling as if every tear of hers tucked his own further and further away.

"Stop saying that." The words were muffled. "If it were a choice, he would have always chosen you to be all right."

Her words caused him physical pain.

Libby straightened slowly, wiping her eyes and nose on the sleeve of her sweater. She was entirely undone, the opposite of how Henry had seen her in the past two years.

She swayed, then clutched the metal railing of his bed. "I… I don't know what to do next. The lawyers were called. The board. I…." Her voice trailed off brokenly. "I just don't know. There are plans…."

"Everything's already spelled out. Father did that years ago," Henry murmured, his stomach and head tight and aching. "The lawyers will take care of it. And I'll… I'll be out of here soon, and I'll take care of it."

Libby shook her head. "You need to rest, Henry. You've been through so much."

"I can rest at home."

There was a slight knock at the door, and Libby rubbed at her eyes. "Oh God, I left him waiting out there. He's anxious to see you."

Henry wasn't paying attention to her; his thoughts were wandering to things he had been trained to think about. The business. His father's legacy. They were his now, and he—not Libby—was the caretaker of WalkCom and the name "Norman Walker" from now on.

Just as he had been bred to be.

"What?"

"He won't believe you're all right until he sees you," Libby said as she walked over to the door. "Won't even stay in his hospital bed."

Henry's gaze focused on Libby, on the door. When it opened and no one came through, he was confused—until she widened it and a wheelchair was eased in.

Archie.

A wave of dizziness pounded into Henry's body. His eyes clamped closed against the mirage, against the miracle.

Archie.

"Thank God." Archie wheeled up beside him. A hand touched his wrist, and Henry barely bit back a sob.

His father was dead, but Archie was here.

LIBBY MURMURED something about coming back later, and Archie heard the door close. Then they were alone.

And Archie let himself go.

"Henry. Open your eyes," he whispered, his voice wet and broken as he clasped Henry's limp hand. "I'm so sorry, so sorry." The grief swamped him, the sheer terror that Henry would blame him—he needed to explain how hard he'd fought, how much he'd tried to get to Henry, to get to Norman, before the men grabbed them. He needed to apologize for getting shot, for getting knocked out. For not doing the one thing he had been hired to do—protect Henry.

"I...." Henry's voice was faint, full of pain.

"I tried, I swear I did," Archie rambled. "I tried to get up. I got part of the license; I called the police."

"Archie." Henry turned his head and opened his eyes, expression filled with agony.

"I'm so sorry about...." His voice trailed off. He'd lost his father when he was sixteen, but really he'd been gone for many years before that, stolen by gambling and drink. Archie didn't grieve his father's death as much as he did his absence. And he still had his mother.

Henry had no one.

Biting his lip, Henry squeezed back weakly against Archie's hand. "His heart," he whispered.

"I know."

"He just...."

"I know. I'm sorry."

"I...." Henry stopped, looking at Archie with a pleading expression. "I don't know what to do."

The chair lurched as Archie pulled himself up with one hand. He couldn't put pressure on his injured leg, could barely keep his balance with all the medication pumped into his system, but right now nothing could keep him from being closer to Henry.

"You rest; you get stronger. Then we'll figure it out," he murmured, leaning down to whisper in his lover's ear.

Henry nodded, breath hitching as his hand reached up to clutch the fabric of Archie's robe. "I have to talk to the man from the FBI."

"He can wait."

"We need to find out who did this—they killed my father," Henry choked out.

"They're dead. All the men who were at the motel." Archie felt his body getting weaker; he sat down on the edge of the bed, taking some of the weight off his leg. "When they went in to rescue you—the SWAT team shot them."

Henry blinked at him, clearly confused. "They're all dead?"

"Yeah. A nurse heard the cops talking." He didn't mention the part where he'd flirted as much as possible with painkillers in his system to get the information, so desperate to know what was going on.

"Oh."

It was a small word, quiet and weak. "So you need to concentrate on getting better. Resting," Archie said again. "Okay?"

Henry blinked up at him, pupils unfocused and hazy. But after a second's pause he nodded, squeezing Archie's hand. "Okay. But—you too. You're hurt."

"Just a graze." Archie brushed it off. "I'm fine, Henry, I promise."

That seemed to produce both damp eyes and a relaxing of Henry's features. The bruising from the accident and subsequent attack had begun to show along his jaw and near his temples—and Archie wished to God those men weren't already dead.

He wanted five minutes with them. That would be all he'd need.

A knock on the door startled them both; Archie automatically moved his body to shield Henry's.

The door swung open, and a dark-suited man stepped in.

"Excuse me—I'm Agent Feller. I was hoping to speak to Mr. Walker."

Archie didn't respond; he turned to look at Henry, searching his face for guidance. He wasn't sure it was his place to send the man away.

Henry nodded, stroking his thumb over Archie's wrist. "It's okay. I'll talk to him. You… you go lie down. Please."

The soft, pleading tone did him in. Archie reluctantly released his hold on Henry's hand—their intimate touch hidden by the bulk of Archie's body—and lowered himself into the wheelchair with a sigh.

"Tell the nurse to come get me if you need anything," Archie murmured, waiting for Henry's tiny smile, waiting for an acknowledgment.

He got both. Only then did he turn to face the man again, his gaze cool. "Excuse me," he said politely, wheeling himself toward the door. The agent opened it, giving Archie ample room to maneuver.

Archie resisted the urge to look back.

Chapter Six

"Mr. Walker—first of all, let me just extend my condolences on your loss," Agent Feller said smoothly, standing tall next to Henry's bed. He'd reintroduced himself and flashed a badge Henry could barely see.

"Thank you."

"I appreciate you speaking with me at such a difficult time, but the quicker we get the information, the better our chances of resolving this case."

Henry struggled to move—everything was beginning to hurt. "I thought they were all dead—the kidnappers. At the motel."

Agent Feller blinked twice, then nodded slowly. "Yes, that's correct." He didn't ask how Henry knew. "We just want to make sure they were the sole perpetrators of the crime."

Henry hadn't thought of that; he stopped struggling and stared at Agent Feller. "What?"

"We just want to make sure there wasn't anyone else involved."

"Oh." Henry felt himself sinking into the mattress. "All right. I'll tell you what I remember, but honestly—it's all a little hazy right now."

"Of course." The older man reached into his pocket and pulled out a small leather portfolio. "Can you tell me what you remember of the past twenty-four hours?"

Henry gave a slightly edited version of events—he skipped over the night spent in the pool house with Archie, because what did that matter?—and cobbled together a few images of the attack on their car and the subsequent captivity at the motel. When he reached the point of the rescue and his father's death, Henry began to choke up.

Agent Feller wrote a few more notes, then nodded. "Can I ask you about your father's staff? Who are the people closest to the day-to-day operations?"

"Uh—Maria DeClavo, his assistant. She's been with him for thirty years. David's his right hand. He's also been with the company since before my father took over."

"At the house?"

"Magnus, the butler. Hilary Keys is the housekeeper."

"Drivers?"

Henry thought longingly of Archie, shuttered away in another room. "Paul Darden drives… drove my father. And then there's Archie Banks."

A pause in the writing, and Agent Feller's gaze locked on to Henry's. "Your bodyguard."

"Well—yes. That's his title." Henry shrugged. "Though until today, we've never had an issue."

An issue. That was the understatement of the century.

"He's armed, though."

"Yes. Father insisted." Ironic it had done absolutely no good.

The agent made a small noise in the back of his throat.

"Mr. Banks—he's worked for you for five years?"

"Well, he's been my bodyguard and driver that long. Before that, he worked at the estate. He… he grew up there. His mother was the housekeeper."

"So he's very acquainted with the way things work during any given day—both at the house and at the office?"

Henry blinked up at the man. "Yes, of course."

"It's common for him to drive your father?"

"No, not really." Henry felt his face contorting into a frown. "It was… it was just how things turned out. My father asked me to come to dinner, so I stayed over at the house. In the morning, we had the meeting. So Archie drove everyone."

"And the route?"

"The route? I don't know. He was taking the back roads to avoid traffic." The headache was coming back at full strength, nausea rising. "Why are you asking these things?"

"Just gathering information." Agent Feller closed the portfolio, tucking the pen in the side. "I'll leave my card if you think of anything else. But I'll be in touch with some follow-up questions regardless."

"Fine." Henry didn't keep the annoyance out of his voice. He closed his eyes, turning his head to one side—away from Agent Feller—clearly indicating the conversation was over.

HENRY FELL asleep, waking twice over the next few hours; a nurse took his vitals, and Dr. Brighton arrived to shine a tiny light in his eyes and ask questions about the date.

"Concussion," the doctor told him. "A pretty serious one. We're going to do a CAT scan in the morning—"

"When can I go home?" Henry cut in. The relentless thoughts about his father—things not done, not said—had given way to a dull calm. There were actions he had to take, and he couldn't take them from this bed.

"I would advise spending a few days here—"

"No." Henry's hands moved restlessly over the blankets; his foot jiggled against the mattress. His gaze darted everywhere but where the doctor stood. "I can rest at home. Unless I'm in danger of dying, I want to go home."

Dr. Brighton huffed out a breath. "After the CAT scan, if everything looks normal, I'll release you."

"Fine. Thank you." The conversation was over.

Norman would have been proud.

LIBBY CAME back in the morning—showered, changed, and neatly put together in a lightweight black sweater and slacks. She carried a large bouquet of orange tulips in a crystal vase.

"Henry, darling, how are you feeling?" she asked, the roughness of her voice the only clue as to how she'd spent the night.

"Sick of this bed," he muttered, cranky and restless after a fitful night of sleep. Terrible dreams and painful memories had tossed him like a tiny boat in a storm for hours. Then he remembered his father was lying in a cold metal drawer somewhere in this building, and his stomach clenched.

"I can imagine," Libby said, placing the vase on the wheeled table near his bed. "I spoke to the doctor. He said you might be able to leave in a few hours."

"Right." Henry sat up with difficulty; his body ached as new bruises seemed to bloom every time he moved.

"Things have been happening. The lawyers called me. David talked to the board as well." Her voice faltered.

"How is David?" God, he felt awful—how had he forgotten about his godfather?

"He's fine. Shaken up. Sad." Libby faced him, done with her flower fussing. She gripped the metal railing with both hands. "As we all are."

Henry reached up to take her hand; he could feel the fine tremors—he wasn't sure if they were hers or his.

"The FBI agent talked to me," Libby said, before he could say anything.

"And?" *Did he ask about Archie?*

"He asked about the staff." She bit her lip. "It was strange. He wanted to know how long Paul and Hilary had been with us."

A strange relief coursed through Henry's body. "It's routine. They need to eliminate the people known to us before they can look outside," he said with far more confidence than he felt.

"Right." Libby sighed. "They're going to talk to everyone, aren't they?"

"Yes."

Her eyes shone with unshed tears as her grip tightened on his fingers. "It's just so terribly upsetting. To imagine anyone, but someone who works for us...."

Henry nodded, unable to voice reassurances. He wanted to believe that beyond a paycheck, the people who worked for his family didn't hate them enough to do something so awful. His father wasn't the easiest man, but he wasn't deserving of death.

"Let's hope they don't find anything," he said eventually. A knock at the door saved him from having to continue with empty platitudes.

ARCHIE ENDURED a prolonged visit from his take-no-shit doctor—a fast-talking woman named Vika Vikari—and her cold hands. She handled his leg under the assumption that the tiny pill he'd swallowed at six in the morning had sufficiently numbed the pain.

It hadn't.

He gritted his teeth as she rebandaged the wound.

"I'm willing to release you this evening provided you don't have a temperature and you promise you'll take it easy. Stay off your feet."

She produced a small light, shining it into his eyes. "How's your vision?"

"Fine."

"Headache?"

"Not bad." It was only a little white lie.

She snapped off the light and regarded him with frank disbelief. "Do you have a place to recover, without stairs, where there will be someone to take care of you?"

Archie thought about his apartment, a fourth-floor walk-up, and his mother's apartment—in the basement but too small for a wheelchair—and nodded, smiling in a way he hoped conveyed sincerity. "I'll stay with my mother. She has a basement apartment. And she'll take care of me." He briefly considered batting his eyelashes.

Dr. Vikara all but rolled her eyes. "Fine. Make sure you set up a follow-up appointment with your physician to check the healing. You should be out of here before dinner."

It was hard not to pump his fist in victory.

She left him alone after that, which meant time to think—a dangerous way to pass the time. Archie couldn't stop thinking about Henry, couldn't stop revisiting the current situation. Norman Walker was dead. And there were dead men in body bags, identities still unknown, who had botched a kidnapping so badly they might have cooked up the plan over breakfast that morning.

When he'd regained consciousness, there was wreckage all around him from the destroyed Hummer. He couldn't go anywhere, couldn't yell for help, but he could lie there and repeat the description in his head, the jumble of letters and numbers he had seen before he'd passed out.

Blue panel van. Midnineties, most likely. J87, maybe a 4. Maybe an R.

Blue panel van. Midnineties, most likely. J87, maybe a 4. Maybe an R.

A passing bakery delivery van had found him twenty minutes later, the young man in the driver's seat frantically calling 911 while approaching Archie with caution. Relief had flooded through Archie as he was assured, yes, the police were coming. *Yes. Don't worry.* They were on their way.

Then the young man had held his wadded-up hoodie against the bloody graze of a gunshot on Archie's left thigh.

All the while Archie's main concern had been Henry. The sheer terror of not knowing where he was or what the kidnapper's intentions were. By the time the paramedics had sedated him, he'd wound himself up into a frenzy of fear.

Where was Henry?

What were they doing to him?

Why hadn't he been able to stop them?

Now, lying in the hospital room, he had more time and a clearer head to think about it.

Eyes closed, Archie examined the events. The ramming of the Hummer—from the right, knocking them off the road into a cluster of trees. The timing was either perfectly estimated or complete luck. It disabled Archie—though that could have been lucky as well.

Norman was sitting in the middle, David to his left and Henry to his right. Was that the usual configuration?

Yes.

When Archie woke up, he was outside the Hummer and already shot. Had they missed when trying to kill him? Was the graze an accident? Why not a second shot?

They took his gun.

They knocked him out, left him injured but not fatally.

Why not take him out?

Archie opened his eyes and stared at the popcorn ceiling of his room. They left him alive, a potential witness. The most trained person in the group, the one most likely to be able to give descriptions.

Why?

He sighed, pulling the blankets up over his shoulder. God knew he was grateful to be alive. Bodyguards usually ended up heroes or dead in situations like that. But it was all so confusing.

The kidnappers—all five of them—were dead at the motel. A motel just five miles from where the grab had taken place. No ransom note, no calls, no demands. It had taken less than an hour to locate the van, the motel, and rescue the hostages.

Why?

HE WOKE up a few hours later when an aide rattled through the door with a tray of food. After she left, a man in a dark blue suit entered through the open door.

"Mr. Banks?" the man asked as Archie pulled the plastic cover off some limp-looking pasta.

"Yes?"

"If you have a second?" The man approached the bed, holding out his identification for Archie to read. "Agent Turner, FBI."

"Oh, of course, come in." Archie covered his food again, pushing the table aside. He sat up quickly, eager to assist the investigation in any way possible. "I was surprised no one talked to me yesterday."

Agent Turner was young and handsome, more like a movie star than a real person. His smile was affable as he moved to stand next to Archie's bed.

"I just have a few questions."

Archie's smile faltered.

"Don't you need my full statement?"

"Not right now." Agent Turner pulled out a tiny spiral notebook and ballpoint pen.

Unease began to creep into Archie's bones.

"IT'S A tragedy," David Silver said, sitting at Henry's bedside. "A goddamn tragedy. I'm glad they're all dead, Henry, I am. Because if they weren't...." His voice broke slightly as he shook his head. The past twenty-four hours had aged the man, aged them all.

"Yes," Henry murmured, because he couldn't think of anything else to say. David had arrived, sat down, and begun to rant in a slightly manic fashion for nearly twenty minutes.

Henry was trapped.

Libby didn't last for more than a few minutes. She and David were polite chitchat sorts; David and Norman were close during the years spanning all the Mrs. Walkers but had only been the best man for Norman and Camille. That said something, the gossips always whispered. David didn't approve of the many wives Norman took, because Henry's mother was his favorite.

"This is on you now, Henry. All of it. The business, the future." His dark-eyed gaze narrowed in on Henry's face. "Everything."

"Of course." Heir apparent, the caption of nearly every photograph in every newspaper and magazine since he was eleven. The next Norman Walker.

It made his head swim.

But he was a grown-up, closing in on thirty, well educated and surrounded by some of the best business minds in the world. He could do this.

Of course, said a small voice in his mind, one of them might have orchestrated the event that killed your father.

"The funeral will be day after tomorrow, the will to be read afterward. It's what your father wanted," David rambled on. "I've put off the board until Monday." He gave Henry a sharp glance. "You'll be up for that?"

"What? Yes, of course. They're releasing me later today."

David rubbed at his eyes with one hand. "Fine. I'm going home. I'll come by tomorrow to see you at the house."

Henry nodded. He accepted the gentle pat against his wrist as a sign of affection, then watched David shuffle out the door.

He'd barely had time to rest when another knock sounded.

"Come in." He sighed, desperate for a nap. Desperate to leave and—what? Go back to his father's house, now to be haunted by two ghosts, two sets of memories of lives gone in an instant?

The door swung open, and the clang of a wheelchair brought the specter of a smile to his face. "Archie."

"Damn this stupid contraption," Archie bitched, but he brightened when he saw Henry. "I asked for crutches, and there was laughter."

"Clearly they haven't seen you trying to maneuver that thing."

Archie freed himself from the door and rolled to Henry's side. "How are you feeling?"

"All right." Henry caught Archie's look, caving pretty quickly. "Except for the headache and the absolute dread of going home. Having to...."

He trailed off, and Archie didn't push. Their hands brushed against one another's, splayed on the mattress.

"Everything must be arranged."

"David said the funeral is the day after tomorrow; they're reading the will right afterward." Henry twitched, restless. He let his fingertips brush against Archie's wrist. "They'll expect me to speak at the service."

"No—not if you don't want to. I think they'll understand if you refuse."

"He'd expect me to speak," Henry said finally. He found only understanding in Archie's expression.

"I can't argue with that."

They sat in silence, almost touching, Henry drawing comfort from Archie just being there, as he had been for so many years. Companion, friend, lover.

"I was so frightened when we were in that room," Henry whispered, gaze trained on the smooth, tanned skin of Archie's forearm, the sprinkling of dark blond hair peeking out from under the robe's sleeve.

"Of course, it must've been terrifying."

"I was... I was afraid you were dead." The words rushed out, bumping into each other on the way from his brain, past his tongue. A cold fear started to creep along his skin—they didn't talk to each other like that. They didn't; they never had.

"Oh."

Henry didn't look up, but then he didn't have to, because Archie was moving, leaning his elbows against the mattress to push up.

His face—gorgeous, even bruised and pale—came to a stop a scant few inches from Henry's, the expression one of utter seriousness.

"All I could think of was where you were and how to find you," Archie whispered.

Henry's heart stuttered. The kiss wasn't smooth or sexy, but the press of Archie's mouth to his was the best thing Henry had felt in his life. Chapped lips and banged-up cheeks and weakened hands—put together, they were glorious and wonderful.

Archie changed the angle just enough to slot them together a bit closer, licking along the seam of Henry's lips. And he didn't hesitate for a second to open his mouth, smothering a moan as their tongues touched.

They didn't do this; they didn't kiss outside of sex.

Or talk.

Or reveal.

Archie cradled Henry, one arm around his back, his hand holding Henry's face as Archie deepened the kiss. Henry's passivity gave way to greediness; he sucked Archie's tongue into his mouth, bringing one hand up to cup the back of Archie's neck.

Everything seemed to spark the next level of heat, of intimacy.

Archie pressed Henry back into the bed, and that was when they both broke the kiss with dual irritated moans.

"Shit, I'm going to end up on the floor." Archie wrenched his arms away, barely catching himself before lowering into his chair. His cheeks were flushed, his lips bitten red, and Henry wished he could crawl into his lap.

Instead he reached out to stroke two fingers over Archie's mouth, drawing a groan from the other man that indicated the best sort of pain. "Come back to the estate with me."

And the unexpected bombing of words continued.

Surprise filled Archie's expression. He looked at Henry, then away, blinking.

"You'll have people to watch over you. Your mum can stay as well—there's plenty of room. The guest suite has everything you need and room enough for the wheelchair." Henry rambled, swallowing between sentences. "And I… I just really need…."

You.

Because Archie knew him too well, he didn't make Henry say the word. Instead he looked at him, smiling, and nodded. "If you're sure it's all right."

"No one will question you recovering at the house," Henry whispered, heart beating triple time. "We'll be discreet."

"Of course," Archie said quickly. He rolled the wheelchair back a few inches as if subconsciously reacting to the reminder; at the house they would be Henry Walker and his faithful, injured bodyguard, Archie Banks. Separate and separated.

Henry despaired. The expectations he'd lived with all his life—the far-off "someday" as Norman's successor—had suddenly exploded into reality. This wasn't someday; this was now.

When the will was read in two days, it would be official.

And the only person who didn't treat him like Norman's son was Archie.

"We'll figure it out."

Archie tipped his head to one side, quizzical as he regarded Henry. A smile finally ghosted over his face.

"You're going to have a lot on your plate," he said gently. "I'll be there if you need anything, but Henry, I don't have any expectations."

"Thank you," Henry whispered, but he didn't mean it at all.

EVELYN BROUGHT Archie a change of clothes. They were a pair, both with their bum legs and unable to move quickly or fluidly. But it was just the two of them, as it had been for most of Archie's life, so today, as she helped him into sweatpants and a T-shirt, it was the status quo.

Except for the fact that Archie had a gunshot graze on his left outer thigh, his boss was dead, and he was headed for the Walker estate to recover.

"You're okay with coming with me to the house?" Archie asked, gingerly wiggling his feet into wool-lined slippers.

"I worked there for twenty-five years, Archie," she said with a huff, pulling a windbreaker from her tote bag. "I can go back for a few weeks."

"I doubt it'll take that long." His voice drifted off. Take that long for what? To feel better? To be done watching out for Henry?

He really had no idea.

"As long as it takes." That was clearly her final word on the matter as she shook the jacket in his direction. "They're sending a car, then?"

"Yes, Mum." Archie put the jacket on, then rested his hands on his lap. Every hour that passed, something began to ache and throb in earnest. He breathed through a pulse of pain.

"We have to stop at a pharmacy, fill the painkillers." Evelyn went into fuss mode, hobbling around on her cane as she gathered Archie's things—a few cards, a bouquet of flowers from Libby Walker—to get ready to go. "Do you need anything from your flat?"

"My laptop." Archie cringed—his schoolwork.

He remembered his interview scheduled for yesterday that he didn't call to change. *Sorry I was foggy with pain and trying to keep my shit together.*

"All right. We'll stop there. You'll stay in the car," she said sternly, flashing him a green-eyed stare.

"Mum, you're not supposed to be moving around so—"

"Think of it as my new therapy," she said, cutting him off. "And hush. I'm your mother—this is my job."

Archie smiled at that, resolving to hold his tongue and let her do at least some things to help him.

"Remember, you're there to help me—keep out of the kitchen," he teased.

She stopped and shot him an impressively withering look. "I'll pitch in where needed," she said diplomatically.

A chime sent Evelyn digging into the pocket of her jacket.

"The car's downstairs, love." She flipped her ancient cell phone shut. "I'll get the nurse."

In the end it took them almost fifteen minutes to get Archie and everything else into the back of the hired limousine. By the time they were on the road to the estate, Archie was exhausted.

And he hadn't had time to see Henry before he'd left.

"It's just so crazy," Evelyn said, catching Archie's attention. She worried her hands in her lap.

"I know." He didn't need to ask what she was referring to.

"I hope it's over and done. And all those horrible men are accounted for." Evelyn sighed; she and Archie reached for each other's hands almost at the same time. "I don't want to imagine there's anyone else out there, thinking such horrible ideas about Henry."

Archie nodded, squeezing his mother's hand.

He had his doubts.

Chapter Seven

Hilary greeted them at the front door with red eyes and wearing head-to-toe black. She and Evelyn embraced as Magnus directed the limo driver on where to carry the luggage. Archie took his time getting into the foyer, bracing himself for the rush of people fussing over him.

"A hero," Magnus blustered, holding his arm and leading him to the first-floor guest suite in the back of the house. "If you need anything, Archie, anything at all." The elderly butler barely made it to Archie's sternum, and he tried not to lean any of his weight on the man lest he crush him.

"I'll be fine." Archie collapsed on the bed with a sigh. The suite had a small bedroom, sitting room, and en-suite bath, all done in dark grays and Tiffany-blue accents. A large arrangement of white roses sat on the dresser. The guest room he'd coveted once upon a time. "Honestly, Magnus. I need a day or two off my feet, and then I can be of some help to you."

Magnus tutted his disapproval. "Mrs. Walker gave us specific instructions, young man—you are to be treated as a guest, and there will be no working, nothing but resting until her private physician examines you."

The man's stern visage made it clear he was not to be messed with, particularly when Hilary and Evelyn came into the room. Archie was incredibly outnumbered.

"Good to hear it, Magnus." Evelyn let go of Hilary's arm and settled herself into a floral armchair in the corner. She sighed, and Archie knew her leg was bothering her. "Of course I am fully avail—"

Hilary didn't let her finish. "While I'm sure everyone will appreciate you supervising, you're not here to work either, Evelyn—just to relax and be with Archie."

"Now, with all the visitors we'll be having in the next few days—"

"Supervising," Hilary reminded. She patted Archie on the foot gently. "Mrs. Walker was adamant. You're guests."

A weird silence descended over the room then; did they talk about what had happened? Evelyn broke the hush first—she sighed dramatically, shaking her head.

"Too much death in that child's life," she said sadly. Magnus nodded.

"Seems like just yesterday we were dealing with Mrs. Walker's passing."

"Twenty-one years ago? Twenty-two?" Magnus seemed to be thumbing through the endless calendar of his memories, eyes far away. "Henry was just a little thing."

"We were five, or close to it." Everyone looked at Archie, so he contemplated the woven pattern of the gray comforter. "Father and I had just come over from London."

He had been terrified to be in a new country but oh so glad to see his mother again after a two-year absence. Living with his grandmother wasn't the worst thing. His father had stopped by occasionally to check on him, and he and Evelyn talked frequently on the phone. They'd left the tiny flat above the bakery and moved across the ocean, into a grand house where the "servant's quarters" were a great luxury compared to where they had come from.

After being hugged half to death by his weeping mother, Archie had been bathed, redressed in clean, new clothes, and brought to the main hall to meet the Walkers. The disinterested Norman, the blonde and ethereal Camille, and tiny Henry, who hid behind his mother's skirts at the sight of a boy his age. He wouldn't come out fully, just occasionally peeking with one blue eye while the adults conversed.

Archie had been impatient with the little boy—weren't they to be playmates? Didn't he want to run around in the great spaces that surrounded this amazing house?

Two weeks later Norman was in Hong Kong, Camille was dead, and Evelyn had Archie on her knee, pushing the hair out of his eyes.

"Henry's lost his mum—you must be gentle with him," she'd said sadly.

NOW, TWENTY-FIVE years later, Henry had lost his father.

And Archie wanted to be gentle with him. He wanted to protect him from what was to come.

His mother's voice cut through his hazy memories, and he shook away the cobwebs. "Come on; let's leave him to a nap."

"I'm sorry."

"Stop, stop. I'm going to the kitchen to have Hilary serve me tea, seeing as I'm a guest," Evelyn said drily. "You sleep. We'll bring you soup later."

Magnus helped her to her feet. She shuffled over to the bed to drop a kiss on Archie's cheek.

"Thanks, Mum." He smiled at her gratefully. "Wake me when Henry gets home—please?"

She didn't question why, just nodded. She ran her fingers over the soft fuzz of his buzz cut, lost, it seemed, in her own memories.

Just like old times.

Unfortunately.

HENRY SLEPT the distance from the hospital to the house; Libby roused him when they arrived, petting his arm gently. Outside it was getting dark, the sky a dark blue streaked with orange.

The driver helped him out of the car; he wanted to shake the man's hovering hands off, but that would require the world to stop spinning.

It wasn't.

"Hilary texted me—Archie and Evelyn are here, all settled in. I put him in the guest suite on the main floor, and Evelyn is staying in the room next to Hilary." Libby prattled on, balancing her purse and the large vase of flowers. The manic edge stretched from her voice to the tremor in her hands. "The caterers have been called for the reception tomorrow, after the… funeral." Her voice cracked as she walked toward the door. "I didn't want Hilary to have to manage so much, with guests and all."

Henry leaned on the driver's arm, letting the man guide him. "Good idea," he said. Archie was here; he wanted to see Archie.

At the top of the stairs, Magnus appeared, clucking over Libby holding the vase, relieving her of it with demanding hands. "Madam, please allow me."

"Thank you." Libby whirled around, reaching for Henry's arm. "I'll get you upstairs to bed, check with Hilary on dinner."

"Libby, take a breath. Please." Henry looped his arm around her waist. "Please."

She stopped talking, but the vibrating jitters continued to rack her body. Henry thought he should speak to the family doctor, see about getting her something to calm her nerves.

They went through the front door, and Henry blinked—the lights were all on, seemingly every light in the house. Hilary was standing at attention near the bottom of the stairs, dressed in her official uniform, the one that was only brought out for special events held at the house. Magnus, he realized, was also wearing his formal suit. He stood next to Hilary, chin up. Next to him, in a simple blue dress and with her hair pulled back, was Evelyn, gazing at him with love and sympathy.

Henry wanted to cry.

"We just wanted to welcome you home, Mr. Walker, and the staff expresses their deepest condolences on the loss of your father," Magnus said, stiff and proper even as his eyes got damp. "We are here for whatever you may need."

"Thank you," he said softly, releasing the driver's arm to walk over to them. He managed it with some success—he didn't end up on the floor at least.

He shook Magnus's hand and accepted a sad nod from Hilary. When he reached Evelyn, he didn't bother with protocol; he leaned down and gave her a hug.

"Poor sweet boy," she whispered. "I'm so sorry."

"Is Archie all right?" He lowered his voice as much as he could.

"Sleeping. He'll be fine." Evelyn pulled back. She reached up to pat his cheek tenderly. "You being home will speed his recovery."

They think we're friends, just childhood friends, Henry thought, trying not to read anything into Evelyn's words—or the strange expression on Libby's face when he turned around.

"Thank you all for your support," Libby said, suddenly composed. "Henry, why don't you go upstairs and lie down? Hilary will bring you dinner."

He considered saying he wasn't hungry, but there was pretty much no way that excuse was going to work with these four people. Henry squeezed Evelyn's hand, then moved toward the stairs.

"Soup," Evelyn called after him. "You're getting soup and tea."

"I'd expect nothing else," he murmured, casting her a small smile before concentrating on the seemingly endless flight of stairs above him.

DESPITE THE exhaustion and dizziness, Henry managed to get undressed and into bed without incident. Everything smelled better here; everything was normal and comforting and familiar.

And that was when it hit him, really, truly hit him.

It wasn't normal anymore.

Normal was strangers committing violence against his family. Normal was watching his father struggle to breathe and listening to apologies because no one could save him. Normal was this constant sense of dizziness and pain that racked his head. Normal was his life now belonging to WalkCom.

He pressed his face into his pillow, unable to stop the tears trickling down his cheeks.

He wanted five minutes, just five. Just enough to tell his father that despite everything, he loved him. That he understood his father's world had collapsed when his mother died. How were you expected to go on when everything that kept you moving was gone?

Your motivation.

Your inspiration.

Gone.

Henry cried for a little while, for his father and his mother and maybe even for himself. When he was out of tears, he rolled over to the dry pillow and fell into a dreamless sleep.

Chapter Eight

THE PROCESSION of cars pulled into the driveway of the estate, the limo carrying Henry, Libby, David, and Rebecca Silver in the lead. Rebecca and Libby were talking in hushed tones while David checked his phone. A dull headache throbbed behind Henry's eyes as he rested against the seat, head tilted to stare out the window. The graveside ceremony was rough, as difficult as the service had been. The finality of a funeral, the reality that this was the end of the public display. Everything from here on would be private pain and quiet mourning.

The door opened, the hired limo driver letting in the sunlight and warmth to counter the chill of the air-conditioning.

"Thank you," Rebecca said politely, accepting his hand to step out. David was next, and finally Libby, who patted his arm before leaving the limo.

"Sir?"

"Henry? The lawyers are here," David called, and Henry couldn't delay his exit a second longer. Time to greet the mourners who had been invited to the house. Time to hear the will, and make his transition to CEO official.

It was time.

"Thank you," he murmured, scooting across the seat as his head continued to ache. He accepted the man's help, emerging to the sound of subdued chatter from the mourners. At the end of the line of cars, Henry spotted Archie, literally head and shoulders above everyone else. He'd driven to the grave site with his mother, Magnus, Maria, and Kit. Now the little group was talking quietly. Despite being in the same house, they hadn't had a chance to see each other in the past thirty-six hours. Disorientation kept Henry in bed; a fever confined Archie to his room.

Then the streams of visitors and preparation for the wake, setting the house into a tizzy. Henry felt as if he were drowning in the perpetual motion of the people around him.

"Henry?" Libby this time.

"Yes, I'm coming."

"The lawyers are set up in the study."

He took her arm, feeling the tremors racking Libby's body as he tucked her in close. They walked up the steps slowly, the weight of the day wearing on them both.

Mr. Dunlop and Mr. Harvey were fussing with portfolios, murmuring to each other, as Henry and Libby entered the study. Chairs had been pulled into a semicircle around his father's desk, ten in total. Henry felt a wave of nostalgia and sadness—he would never be here again with his father. He would never have the chance to alter the endless cycle of disapproval and resentment they were locked into.

"You should sit down; it's been such a long day already," Libby whispered, nudging him toward a comfortable damask-covered wingchair in front.

"Mr. Walker," Mr. Dunlop said, just noticing they had entered. He hurried over to shake Henry's hand. "We'll be ready to start as soon as everyone arrives."

It didn't take long—an anxious young man in a dark suit appeared at the door, urging the crowd behind him to take their seats.

Henry, seated already, watched them enter.

David and Rebecca Silver, Magnus, Maria… then Evelyn, leaning on Archie as much as he was leaning on her.

He sat up a little straighter as the lawyers' assistant shut the door behind them.

"Mr. Albus and Mr. Seamus were unable to attend. They'll be contacted afterward," Mr. Dunlop announced. Henry nodded, but his gaze never left Archie.

Archie settled his mother into a chair, then limped to the one closest to it.

What were Archie and Evelyn doing at the will reading?

He expected a token for Evelyn—she had been a fixture in their lives for over twenty-five years. There was a list of former employees that would receive a small cash gift of appreciation from his father's estate. This reading, however, was for the large bequeathals.

Was Archie just here to accompany his mother?

Evelyn realized Henry was staring in their direction, and gave him a small wave, her face masked in sympathy. He nodded, smiled—flashed back to his childhood, when he'd realized he had no mother, and his father hadn't been home for days. Evelyn had been there each time, to wipe his eyes and cuddle him on her lap. He associated her with comfort—safety. And a quick glance at Archie, tall and composed at her side, made him feel the same things. Things he absolutely needed at this time.

Libby was saying something; Henry turned back to her, focusing his attention.

"They're starting, Henry," she said again, sniffling back a few tears.

"Yes, of course. Gentlemen, please proceed." It was now his place to say such things; they fell from his lips naturally, like breathing. Like he didn't have to think for them to happen.

His father's lawyers—*his lawyers, his lawyers*—started off with a tag-team rendition of welcome and a host of legal jargon. Henry tuned out, letting his head fall back against the chair; it gave him the ability to look around the room, glancing at each face.

There was sadness. Curiosity.

Archie was already facing his way, as if waiting for Henry's gaze to reach him. His breath caught, a soft sound he covered with a quiet cough. Archie looked down at the floor, then back up to the lawyers, pretending to pay attention.

Henry knew that look. It was the one he'd worn during countless scoldings, warnings, and lectures during their childhood—the ones he endured when taking the blame for whatever mischief Henry had gotten into, for which Archie paid the price. No one would believe the sweet little prince misbehaved; must be the drunk's son.

"We'll start with the smaller bequests," Mr. Harvey said a bit more loudly, as if trying to redirect Henry back into the present. It worked; Henry smiled and nodded.

Magnus was called on first. He struggled to stand, something Mr. Dunlop tried to discourage, but his words trailed off into a throat clearing.

Also, Magnus's first name was Harold.

Magnus had a first name.

"Mr. Walker wanted to thank you for your many years of loyal service to this house, and to the family," Mr. Harvey said, directing his comments

The Heir Apparent

toward the elderly man. "You have been an exemplary employee." He peered at the paper in his hands more closely. "Mr. Walker leaves to you, in addition to your pension and lifetime medical care, the sum of twenty-five thousand dollars."

Magnus made a choking sound, bringing a white handkerchief to his nose as he tried to maintain his stoic visage. Evelyn Banks reached up to pat his arm, murmuring soothing sounds as he sat heavily in his seat.

"A great man, a great man," Henry could make out as their butler wiped his eyes, still muttering.

"Yes." Mr. Dunlop gestured toward Evelyn next.

"I won't be standing," she said.

Henry swallowed a grin.

"Of course. Mrs. Banks. Mr. Walker wanted to thank you for your years of valuable service to the family. Specifically your devotion to Henry, his beloved son."

The air in the room disappeared; everyone seemed to inhale deeply at once, then hold in utter shock at the sentimentality.

Mr. Dunlop continued on. "Your love and caring for Henry was not based on the expectations of your position or salary but from your heart. And he thanks you."

The pause allowed everyone to exhale; Henry blinked until he could focus. He watched Magnus and Archie pat a sniffling Evelyn as she nodded.

"Mr. Walker leaves to you the sum of fifty thousand dollars, in addition to your pension, and the payment of your medical expenses for the rest of your natural life."

Evelyn cried louder than Magnus, weeping openly into the wad of tissues in her hand. Archie leaned close, whispering in his mother's ear as she fell apart.

Henry resisted the urge to go over and hug the woman who was— for all intents and purposes—his surrogate mother.

Mr. Harvey cleared his throat loudly. "The next bequest is for Archie Banks."

David made a sound this time, shifting in his chair. It was almost derision, and Henry snapped his gaze to his godfather. The older man looked away as Rebecca patted his leg.

What the hell did David care?

"Mr. Banks, Mr. Walker wanted to thank you for your service. Not only for the years you've served as an employee, but also for being Henry's companion when you were children."

Henry and Archie locked gazes, snicking together like magnets.

"Your devotion to Henry, your allegiance to the Walker family, and your honorable decision to repay your father's debts impressed him greatly. And he would like you to know your student loans will be paid in full, and you will receive a stipend of twenty-five thousand dollars per year for the next ten years."

Archie gasped, and Henry felt the utter shock and surprise down to his bones. Norman had never seemed to notice Archie, let alone take the time to consider him an honorable man. And this was beyond a thank-you—it gave Archie a clean slate, without student loans, without the need to take a job he didn't want. The yearly stipend would give him freedom to choose a job he wanted. Build a nest egg. Buy a home.

It was beyond generous.

Somehow Mr. Harvey was still talking. Maria this time. Her pension plus a one-time gift of twenty-five thousand dollars, and paid medical expenses for the rest of her life. Henry didn't see her reaction, didn't hear anything. All he could do was stare at Archie.

His devotion. To Henry.

Not the Walker family.

Henry.

Could his father have known? The thought slammed into him unbidden. Then his brain was off and running, sorting through every memory he could pull up.

"Mr. Walker—Henry." Mr. Harvey's voice interrupted his manic stream of consciousness. "Are you all right?"

"Yes," he said automatically. "Just a little dizzy."

The room seemed to twitch as one.

"Gerald? Pour Mr. Walker a glass of water, please."

"You can continue," Henry whispered as the young man in the suit scurried to the back of the room.

"Of course." Mr. Harvey cleared his throat. "To Liberty Frank Walker. There's a separate letter for you," he said kindly. "His bequest is one million dollars, as well as your jewelry, clothing, vehicle, and the house in Maui."

Libby shook her head, dazed. Henry wasn't sure if she was disappointed or overwhelmed. He realized a second later it didn't say anything about the estate or her living there.

David and Rebecca were next.

"David, you have been my closest friend and trusted confidante for thirty years. I could not have achieved the success of WalkCom without you. Therefore I bequeath to you a permanent seat on the board of directors, until you are so inclined to retire. In addition to your pension, my gift to you and Rebecca is one million dollars and the apartment in Rome."

Rebecca sniffed loudly, and David bowed his head. His shoulders were stiff, his neck flushed bright red.

Henry leaned over to pat his godfather on the shoulder. How he must be feeling his mortality, hearing the last will and testament of his closest friend.

The man turned his head, just a flash, and Henry saw anger.

Then sorrow.

They shared a moment, and then Henry leaned back. From across the room, he caught Archie's gaze.

"And lastly we are left with the final bequest, and that is for Mr. Norman Henry Walker, III"

Gerard finally made his presence known, coughing to get Henry's attention. He handed over a large glass tumbler of water.

"Thank you."

Henry concentrated on the water and let Mr. Harvey's voice roll over him.

"To my only son and heir, Henry, I leave the following: the Walker estate and all its lands and possessions. The vehicles, the plane...." Mr. Harvey paused. "There's a listing of everything, Henry, for your edification."

Henry nodded, growing more and more numb.

"As to the matter of WalkCom, Henry will assume the duties of president and CEO...."

There it was. The future he had been groomed for.

"… providing a majority vote is reached by the board of directors."

Henry shook his head. The water sloshed over the sides of the glass, splashing into his lap.

"What?"

No one in the room moved.

Mr. Harvey looked at his partner for some support, then turned back to face Henry.

"According to the will, the board of directors will vote on whether or not you will be installed as president and CEO."

Chapter Nine

Archie couldn't catch his breath after the will reading. The fever that had flared up left him light-headed, but the revelations in Norman's study—he was lucky he could still stand.

Or sit, rather, because they were in the kitchen, perched on stools around the island. Magnus, Evelyn, Kit, and Maria—all slumped over their cups of tea as Hilary buzzed around, putting together a bit of lunch.

Everyone else was eating a catered meal in the dining room.

"Hilary, can I give you some help?" Evelyn called, breaking the awkward silence.

Archie could see Hilary was about to decline, but she smiled at him from across the room, where she sliced a loaf of home-baked bread on a board.

"Oh, Evelyn, that would be lovely. Could you finish with the bread while I put the meat on a platter?"

Magnus muttered something about being stuck in the back room—Archie knew he wanted, needed to be out there, working. But Libby had insisted they take a few hours off, letting the catering staff handle things instead.

It was driving him crazy.

Maria sat politely in the chair, hands in her lap. No one knew her very well, and no one felt comfortable talking about the shocking end to the will reading. He and Kit had been exchanging looks since everyone had been shuffled out of the room, listening to Henry and David talking loudly with the lawyers.

The will made no sense. Where it should have been completely straightforward—Henry got everything—it was just one surprise after another. Including the bequest to Archie.

His head was still spinning, and it wasn't the fever.

Kit sipped her coffee loudly, catching his attention. "I need a quick breath of air," she said suddenly. "Archie? Care to join me?"

She couldn't have been more obvious, and Archie couldn't have been more grateful.

"Excellent plan. We can step out the back door."

He didn't spare a second to check out the expressions on Maria's or Magnus's faces; he dodged his mother and Hilary with his head down, his limp keeping him from moving too fast. He just followed Kit's tiny figure and her flaming red hair across the kitchen, then out the back door.

In the distance he saw the pool house.

How much had changed in seventy-two hours.

"Oh my God," Kit huffed, throwing herself in the Adirondack chair tucked around the other side of the herb-garden pots. Hilary had clearly made herself a quiet nest. "Seriously—oh my God."

"That about sums it up." Archie leaned against the side of the pergola.

"I can't believe Mr. Walker is dead. Or that… that will!" Kit did a crazy wave thing with both hands over her head. "It's insane."

Kit had been waiting for them as they left the room. She heard the commotion.

She cornered Archie with the snap and aggression of an angry teacup poodle.

"Why would he do that?"

"No clue." Archie sighed.

"How can we help him?" Kit looked at him helplessly. "He must be… I can't even imagine."

"We have to watch his back. If the board is going to vote—well, not everyone is going to bend to the obviousness of Henry taking over. There are people on that board who want to be CEO." Archie shook his head.

"I'm back in the office tomorrow. I'll definitely keep my ears open for gossip." She shook her head. "And there's going to be a shitload."

"Can you call me when you hear anything? Just keep it between us for now." Archie caught her expression; as far as she knew, he and Henry were close friends since childhood, and he was now a devoted employee. "I don't think we should upset him."

"Right. He's already pretty overwhelmed."

They sat silently until a rap on the door startled them. Hilary opened the door and peeked out.

"Sorry—lunch is ready."

"Thank you, Hilary." Archie straightened, trying to ignore the twinge and the headache and faint burning in his cheeks. He had things to pay attention to, and how he felt wasn't on that list right now.

MARIA AND Kit were driven back to the city in the hired limo.

Everyone else had left. The caterers cleaned and departed as Hilary supervised a few temporary workers in tidying up.

Archie lingered in the hallway outside the kitchen, sitting in a purloined chair as he rested his leg. His mother was off to her room for a nap, and Magnus patrolled the house, looking for things out of place.

Henry was absent from all this. Archie couldn't even pretend he wasn't waiting for him—he just sat and smiled and watched.

Two hours later and the man of the house finally appeared.

He looked ten years older—suit wrinkled and tie askew. When he emerged from the foyer, he spied Archie and stopped in his tracks.

It was hard to read Henry's expression, but Archie did his best.

He looked exhausted.

"I'm not even going to lie," Archie said softly. "I was waiting for you."

Henry opened his mouth to speak but shut it a second later. He gestured up the staircase.

Archie shook his head, inclining his head toward the guest suite in the back.

A tiny smile ghosted across Henry's face.

They both moved slowly, keeping a healthy distance between them as they made their way down the small hallway toward Archie's temporary rooms. No words, just a quick, furtive glance to make sure no one was around to see where they were going. Together.

"Sit down before you fall down," were the first words Archie said after they were safely in the sitting room, door shut and locked behind them. He spoke to Henry's back, waiting for his lover to turn around.

"I feel like if I stop moving, I won't be able to start again," Henry said, his voice sounding defeated.

Archie limped over. He hesitated, then laid his hand against Henry's shoulder.

Henry trembled.

"Come on," Archie whispered. He maneuvered Henry with gentle nudges until Henry turned and then sat down on the small settee with a thump.

When Henry looked up at him with wide blue eyes, Archie felt his heart turn over.

"Join me?"

Archie didn't hesitate; he settled down with a tiny moan, the pulling strain of the bandage on his thigh making him uncomfortable.

"You shouldn't be walking around on your leg so much," Henry scolded mildly, pushing up against Archie's body as he did.

"Only way to walk around." Archie spread his arm on the back of the couch, just shy of a hug. He regarded his lover with a serious expression. "Are you all right?"

"No."

"What can I do?"

Henry tipped his head to one side, regarding him quizzically. "What can you do?"

"There must be something. This is all a mess. What's your plan with the board?"

He stiffened in response, dragging his gaze to the painting of lilies on the opposite wall. "What can I do? I'll let them decide what my father couldn't."

Archie brushed his fingers over the back of Henry's neck, the thin strip of skin between his hair and the collar of his shirt and jacket. He didn't have an immediate response to Henry's words, not one that wouldn't take Henry's dead father to task.

"You have to make your case—if you want to."

Henry turned to look at him, his forehead wrinkled. "What do you mean?"

"I mean, if you truly want to be the head of WalkCom, you have to convince the board you're the right man for the job. It'll earn their respect."

Or you could walk away, he thought.

"I could do that," Henry said, his voice neutral as he looked to the painting. He slumped into the back of the couch, melting a little against Archie's side.

"Think about that tomorrow," said Archie, pulling Henry closer. At some point the boundaries would come into play, and he would have to stop touching his lover—but today wasn't that day. "Do you want to lie down?"

"This is fine."

"Bed might be more comfortable."

Henry lifted his head, fixing his dark blue gaze on Archie's face. "Yes."

Archie limped and Henry shuffled. They made it into the small bedroom in silence, not quite looking at each other.

"Get your suit off." Archie took charge because he didn't know what else to do. And Henry looked lost.

"Someone might…."

Archie didn't respond; he undid his tie, then stripped off each piece of his suit, throwing it on the floor. The pants were rough going since his thigh was throbbing. There was a faint pink stain in the center of the bandage, indicating he'd been on his feet too long.

"Oh God," Henry murmured. Archie turned around to find Henry staring at him, horrified.

"What…."

Henry just walked over, eyes never leaving the covered wound on Archie's leg.

"It's okay."

But Henry reached down to touch the edges of the bandage, stroking reverently.

"Henry."

When he dropped to his knees, Archie's mouth went dry.

When Henry pressed his mouth to trace where his fingers had been, Archie cradled Henry's head between his hands.

He swallowed, trying to keep his emotions in check, but in the hours since the kidnapping Archie couldn't stop them from flowing out. Couldn't stop touching Henry.

And Henry seemed to feel the same way. He rubbed his cheek up Archie's thigh, wrinkling the fabric from Archie's boxers as he moved. When Henry's lips grazed the hard line of his erection through the fabric, Archie moaned faintly.

"You don't have to…."

"Shhhh," Henry whispered, his breath caressing the length, which throbbed under the promise of a kiss, a touch.

He reached up for the waistband; carefully he pulled them down over Archie's erection, down to his thighs—oh so careful moving past the bandage. Archie shook with the tender attention being paid to his body.

Usually Henry offered and Archie took.

For years, that had been the way they'd fucked.

But this was something else entirely.

"You're so beautiful, Archie," Henry murmured, as if hypnotized by the long length of his lover's body. He braced his hands on Archie's hips, leaning forward to lick a stripe up his cock.

Archie trembled.

"So brave." Another long swipe of his tongue, this time ending with a twirling twist over the head.

"So patient." Henry wrapped one hand around the base of Archie's dick, warm and tight as he squeezed. "So dear to me." When he took Archie in his mouth, it was almost too much. Archie felt himself swaying with the perfect pleasure of it.

He kept himself still through sheer force of will; he was mindful of Henry's trauma and injury, aware that letting go right now would leave them both on the floor.

But oh God, it hurt so good. The slick wetness of Henry's mouth, the fingers curled around his base, the warm palm sliding over his hip and ass with curious abandon.

"Henry, Henry," Archie choked out, hips rocking as he tried in vain to hold off. When he pulled back, Henry roughly pulled him closer, swallowing him down.

It was a battle of wills, but Archie was already losing. Henry demanded his orgasm wordlessly, and Archie never could say no.

He gasped as he came, a stuttering movement of his hips as Henry drank him down, milking every drop until Archie's knees buckled.

Archie slid to his knees, ignoring the twinge. He couldn't stop the need to kiss Henry, to pull the taste of his own orgasm off his lover's tongue.

"So fucking amazing," Archie murmured, wrapping his arms around Henry's torso. The kiss was wet and rough, teeth and tongue battling for dominance. He wanted to tear Henry's clothes off; he wanted to lay him on the bed and make love….

"Please," Henry whispered as he broke the kiss. His hips rutted against Archie's thigh—it was impossible to miss the meaning.

"Come here." Archie stood with difficulty, pulling Henry with him. He went to work on his clothing, with Henry's trembling hands joining him in the disrobing. Everything was shed in a matter of seconds, until Henry's naked body was revealed.

The bruises hadn't faded.

All the tenderness in Archie's heart bled out; he eased Henry onto the bed, mindful of the bruises. There was only one thing he could think of, and that was making sure Henry knew how much he was adored.

Archie lay over him, stretching to his full height until they were lined up—lips to lips, cock to cock. The gasp beneath him spurred him on; Archie's hips began to move, rubbing their bodies together.

Henry moaned, eyes closed and head thrown back. Archie feasted on the gorgeous curve of his neck, biting at Henry's Adam's apple as he increased his thrusts.

"Come on, baby, come on," he whispered, licking up to Henry's ear. "Just let go."

A few more strokes—Henry's cock rough and dry against Archie's stomach—until Henry let go, truly. He arched, a wet spurt between their bodies signaling his release.

"Archie," Henry gasped, a damp sigh against his lover's shoulder.

"I'm here. I'm right here," Archie whispered back, shielding Henry from the rest of the world, body and soul.

Chapter Ten

"It's good to see you," Kit said as Henry got out of the car. Four days since the will reading, nearly a week since the kidnapping, and he'd finally convinced Libby and Evelyn to let him venture past the front gate.

Henry smiled, let her take his briefcase as her hands hovered nervously. Paul had the same expression on his face—concern—as he held open the door.

Everyone was waiting for Henry to crumple to the ground.

Which was why he pushed his shoulders back as he walked toward the building, Kit trotting along at his side.

"Did you schedule everything I asked you to?"

"Yes." The slight hesitation in her voice gave him pause as they stepped through the doors.

"What's wrong?"

Kit's gaze dropped to his shoes.

"Can we... we talk about it upstairs?" she murmured.

Henry nodded, putting his hand on her elbow to guide her to the elevator that much more quickly. He exchanged polite smiles and subdued greetings with the security guards and front-desk staff, all the while aware of Paul shadowing him and Kit fidgeting at his side.

There wasn't a second he could pretend this was just another day at the office.

The elevator ride was silent; Neil didn't even turn around. They exited on the executive floor, where all activity seemed to cease—and all the sound disappear—as Henry stepped into the reception area.

A small crowd gathered, almost by accident, it seemed. People walking by stopped and stared.

Henry felt the expectation growing.

"Good morning," he said, nodding to acknowledge their stares. "We've all suffered a great loss, of an irreplaceable man. But he taught us all well, didn't he? Let's see if we can't keep this place running in tip-top shape." He smiled, or at least attempted to. A few people reflected that back, while others dropped their gazes and scurried back on their way.

He sighed inwardly.

"Let's go," he said to Kit, heading toward the left hallway.

Then realized she wasn't following him.

"Um—I thought you might be in the other office," Kit said slowly, her cheeks turning a flaming red. "Your...."

"I know what you meant." It came out harsher than he wanted it to, and that immediately showed in her expression. "Sorry. Let's just—I'd rather be in my office for right now."

Kit nodded. Henry turned on his heel and strode quickly down the hallway to the small suite of offices he shared with Kit.

They didn't talk again until they were in Henry's office. He ignored the multitude of flower arrangements, spilling out to Kit's desk, and dropped into his chair with a sigh.

"What's wrong?"

"I called the board members. Out of the twelve, only four would agree to meetings. Those are on your calendar. Three refused outright. The rest said they would get back to me." Kit's words came out in a frantic rush.

"They know about the will." Henry leaned back, already exhausted. His head pounded while red flicks of anger began to build. "They know about the fucking will, and since I'm a lame-duck president, they don't have any urgency to respond."

Kit leaned back, as if distancing herself from his harsh words.

"I'm calling an emergency board meeting. Tomorrow. Nine a.m. No proxies—everyone needs to be there."

"Yes, sir." Kit stood.

"Where's David?"

"Mr. Silver is working from home today."

Henry scowled. "Get legal and public relations in here. I want to know what's going on."

"Yes, sir."

He waved her off, instantly regretting his tone as the door closed behind her. He and Kit had always maintained a good relationship—friendly and easygoing, with a healthy sense of humor. Now he was acting—well, he was acting like Norman, a thought that sliced him twice, with shame and sadness in equal measures.

Archie was still on bed rest, his persistent fever having come back with a vengeance. The doctor wouldn't clear him to work, and with the double team of Evelyn and Hilary, he had little chance of getting away from the house anytime soon.

Henry, in his selfishness, desperately wanted him here.

He took his iPhone out of his pocket, scrolling to find Archie's number. But before he could make the call, his desk phone rang.

"Yes?" Henry tried to school his voice into politeness despite the flare of anger at being disturbed.

"Agent Feller with the FBI is here to see you," Kit said nervously through the speaker.

"Fine, send him in." Henry dropped his phone on the desk.

The door opened, and Agent Feller entered. That same tie. The same irritating smile.

"Mr. Walker. Sorry to disturb you."

"An appointment would work better." Henry didn't offer to shake his hand. He gestured toward his visitor chair. "What can I do for you?"

"We've finished our preliminary investigation and believe there was a person working on the inside, feeding information to the kidnappers."

Henry's blood went cold.

"Do you have a name for me?"

"No. Not yet." Agent Feller crossed his legs. "But I have some ideas."

"Are you going to share them?"

"How well would you say you know Archie Banks?"

Henry laughed rudely. Loudly.

"Try someone else. Archie had nothing to do with this."

"You're sure."

"Absolutely."

"He fits the profile of the person I believe we're looking for."

He sounded convinced.

Positive.

"Then you're looking at the wrong profile. Archie could have been killed by those men. That bullet could have torn an artery. He could have bled to death on the pavement. Not to mention it was the information he provided that led you to the motel." Henry's anger mounted. "Unless you have another name or black-and-white proof, I don't want to hear this theory again."

Agent Feller didn't even blink. "I need to ask you to open your household to my agents. We'd like to check accounts, phone logs." The change of conversation was smooth.

Henry shrugged. "Whatever you need to do. I have nothing to hide."

Except he did.

A whisper of fear went through him.

Couldn't he just say, Archie and I are lovers. I know he didn't have anything to do with it because I trust him with my life.

The urge to do it pushed him, but it quickly died into fear.

The board was turning their back on him, and a chink in his armor would be suicide.

"Call the house and talk to Hilary; she's the housekeeper. She'll arrange for whatever you need."

"Thank you so much." Agent Feller rose, the haughty smile in place. "May I also speak to your assistant about records from your office?"

"Of course."

Henry turned his chair, reaching for the receiver as he gave the agent a dismissive glare. "Thank you."

"I'll be in touch."

When he was gone, Henry knocked a decorative globe to the floor in a quick sweeping motion.

ARCHIE SLEPT all day, waking only to receive tea and water from his ever-present mother. At four the doctor came again, examining his wound and taking his temperature.

"A slight infection," he pronounced. "Another few days and you should be fine. I'm prescribing an antibiotic."

There was no arguing—not with his mother right there—and Archie was resigned to his bed. It was frustrating, mostly because seeing Henry depended on his lover coming to him, and that didn't seem to be happening all that much.

He understood things were difficult at the office, and there was still recovering and healing and grief to work through. He just wanted to not feel so incredibly helpless.

The fever even prevented him from doing his schoolwork, and suddenly his graduation was in jeopardy. If he didn't pass these three classes, he would have to retake them. Another semester seemed like forever at this point.

Edgar Ferelli had sent him an email, expressing condolences and wishing him a speedy recovery. No mention of that interview being rescheduled, or Archie getting another chance.

He deleted it after reading it once.

"Did you email your teachers?" Evelyn asked, pouring his tea into a rosebud-painted cup. The tea tray was full of traditional treats, with the best of the household towels and plates.

"Yes, Mum." Archie managed to sit up.

"Were they understanding?"

Archie smiled. He imagined his mother on the phone with his teachers, demanding he get extra time after what he had been through.

"Yes. I got two weeks."

"That's barely enough time!"

"Mum, it's fine." He took his tea, letting the fragrant aroma calm his nerves.

"Hmm." Evelyn sat in the chair at his bedside, her own cuppa in her hands. "Well, at least you're resting now. That's something."

"I hope to get cleared for work in a few days," he reminded her.

Evelyn barely managed to restrain her exasperated expression. "Yes, yes. You and Henry, so eager to rush back into the fray, no attention paid to your injuries."

"If the doctor says—"

"That doctor isn't your mother."

Well, Archie couldn't argue with that.

A soft knock at the door drew both their attention, and as if he'd heard his name, there stood Henry, pale and smiling wanly.

"I cannot bear to see you looking like that." Evelyn pulled herself out of the chair. "Sit down, now."

"I could get another...."

"Henry Walker, I will not deal with more back talk right now." She gave Archie a dirty look. "Sit."

"Yes, ma'am."

Archie tried not to laugh—if only not to inflame his mother more—as Henry unbuttoned his suit jacket and settled into the chair.

"Tea." It wasn't a question.

"Yes, ma'am."

Henry and Archie shared a look—but Archie couldn't miss his mother's gentle smile hidden behind her hand and a faked cough. Evelyn busied herself at the cart, fixing them each a plate.

Neither of them dared complain.

"I'm going to heat some more water," Evelyn declared, though Archie doubted they'd gone through it all yet. But he wasn't going to stop his mother from giving Henry and him some time alone.

When she'd disappeared out the door, Archie turned his focus entirely on Henry. It was impossible to miss the dark circles under his eyes and faint tremors in his lover's hands.

"How bad was it today?"

"Worse than yesterday, if possible." Henry paused to sip from his cup, carefully balancing his napkin and plate on his thigh. "The board meeting was a disaster. Only five people showed up, despite my directive."

"They're just trying to psych you out."

"Well, they're doing a marvelous job."

They sat quietly, Henry's gaze far-off to an imaginary distance, and Archie's locked on his face.

"The FBI agent was back," said Henry in a flat voice.

"Did he have any news?" Archie asked, curious and careful.

"He thinks...." Henry drew in a sharp breath, turning his head to face Archie. "He thinks it was someone inside."

Archie nodded.

"He thinks...."

"It's me," Archie supplied. "I suspected as much when they talked to me in the hospital."

"You seem awfully calm about this." The cup rattled as Henry set it down on the nightstand. His voice had gone high and tight.

"What should I say? I didn't do anything. I have nothing to hide...." His voice trailed off. "Well, I have nothing to hide when it comes to the kidnapping."

Henry's eyes narrowed; Archie watched his face grow more and more pinched.

"It's not a joke if they find out about us."

"The FBI is not the media, Henry. They're not going to put it on Page Six."

"No, but they might go to other people, ask them if they knew about us. It... it just makes you look bad."

Archie's hand jerked, and the tea spilled onto the coverlet. He barely noticed the heated liquid seeping through to his lap.

"Why does it make me look bad? You're the one sleeping with the help," he snapped.

Henry stood up so fast the plate fell to the floor.

"I have other things to worry about." Henry stormed out of the room, leaving a mess in his wake.

"What the hell?" Archie threw the covers aside, then eased himself onto his feet. The fever kept him off balance, but he managed to walk over the spilled food and then to the sitting room.

Henry was nowhere to be found.

Using the walls to guide him, Archie walked slowly out of the suite, perspiring under the strain. He encountered his mother in the hallway, registered her surprise.

"Why did Henry shoot past me like his tail was on fire?"

"I don't know. He's in a mood," Archie said darkly, leaning against the doorjamb. "Where did he go?"

"To the study. You, however, are going to bed."

"No—I have to... five minutes. Ten. I'll go back to bed right after that, I promise," he negotiated.

"Fine. Ten minutes—if you don't come back, I'm coming for you."
Archie nodded, then set out again to find Henry.

HENRY SAT on the couch, a tumbler of scotch in his hands.

Blowing up at Archie was the last thing he wanted to do—added to his harshness toward Kit today and snapping at Paul, who had taken over driving duties. Even his venom for the FBI agent and the various board members who seemed hell-bent on ignoring him.

He wasn't sure what was wrong.

Maybe this was grief.

Maybe this was long-buried anger coming to the surface.

Henry just wanted five minutes where his head didn't fucking hurt.

"Henry?"

Archie called his name, and Henry drained his glass before turning around. He could see his lover holding on to the doorjamb with white knuckles, clearly paying the price for getting up.

Guiltily Henry got up, rushing to Archie's side.

"You shouldn't be out of bed."

"And you shouldn't be freaking out," Archie countered. But he didn't resist taking Henry's arm.

"I know. It was just a fucking piece-of-shit day."

They walked to the couch slowly, Archie holding tight to Henry's arm.

Once they were settled, Henry took Archie's hand in his.

"I'm sorry."

"Why are you pissed at me? I'm the one the FBI thinks is a fucking criminal." The anger was there—but Henry heard the thread of fear.

"I know. I told him he was crazy. It could be anyone but you."

Archie's blue eyes softened; he squeezed Henry's fingers between his own. "You did?"

"Of course. You're a horrible liar—I'd know if you wanted to kill me," Henry said drily.

A shadow crossed his lover's face.

"What?"

"I don't think that was the point."

"The kidnapping wasn't the point?"

"No. I can't explain it, but… it just doesn't make sense." Archie looked at him, serious as Henry had ever seen him. "I think they were trying to do something else."

"Like scare my father so badly his heart would give out?" Henry murmured.

Archie nodded. "Maybe. Maybe create fear and chaos? I don't know."

"I'm going to have the security department at WalkCom send over some people. Just to keep an eye on things."

"Good idea."

"Maybe hire a food taster," Henry joked.

"My mother and Hilary will take it personally."

"Right, no food taster for the king. Or the lame-duck king, as it were." It was hard to keep the bitterness out of his voice.

"You'll convince them, Henry. I know you will."

Henry leaned forward before he could check himself, pressing his lips to Archie's with a small sound of satisfaction. This was what he'd wanted all day—a kiss. A second to feel safe.

When they broke, Archie rested his forehead against Henry's; they breathed the same air for one glorious instant.

"I have to get back to bed before my mum comes to find me," he said softly. "But you can come tonight if you want."

The hopeful tinge to his voice made Henry warm for the first time that day.

"I'll try. But you need your rest." He sneaked in another kiss before straightening.

Archie nodded. "You know where to find me."

For now, a little voice said in his head, but Henry shook it away.

Chapter Eleven

"Thank you for coming."

Henry stood at the head of the table, staring out at the board of directors of WalkCom, including the senior blowhard himself, Xander Pense.

Some of them had been there since Henry was a child, when he would sit outside the boardroom, playing with Matchbox cars while his father conducted business.

Now he stood before them, trying to convince them he wasn't that child anymore.

They didn't look interested for the most part.

"I'm sorry to make demands on your time like this, but it's a difficult period of adjustment and I want us to resolve things so the future of WalkCom is secure."

Kit had printed his notes in a huge font in deference to the debilitating headaches that had been plaguing him in the past two weeks. He knew he was recovering from a concussion, but there were times the pain made the initial blows to his head pale in comparison.

"It's common knowledge that my father's request was for the board to vote on my future role with the company. To install me as president and CEO, or to give those critical positions to someone else."

He took a breath, scanning their faces once more. Indifference. Interest. Dislike. He saw it all. Most of the members looked over at Xander at least once, trying to gauge his reaction.

Which was nonexistent.

"As you know, this company has been my life's focus since I was old enough to understand what a steel manufacturer did. I assure you, being my father's son, I believe I was still in diapers."

A few laughs. He would take them.

"My education, both in school and within these walls, has always been directed toward running this company. To one day step into my father's shoes. He was a demanding and critical man—and he worked for the company every day of the past thirty years as if he had something to prove. Even when he didn't.

"I have something to prove to all of you. That I can lead as my father did. That I can improve on what he began. That I can make this company a force to be reckoned with in the global market. To that end, I ask for a period of four weeks. In that time, I will present my ideas for the company to each of you, and I will be open to your questions and concerns. At the end of the four weeks, there will be a vote."

Henry paused. "Is that acceptable?"

David Silver—who hadn't looked up from his lap since Henry began his speech—now leaned forward to regard his fellow board members. "I second that request."

"Third," someone said from down the table.

"All in favor," David called.

The motion passed.

Henry gathered his things, then turned and left the room.

"WE'RE GOING to work through the weekend," Henry said, shielding his eyes with his hand as Kit scribbled notes on her pad. "I'll stay at my apartment; you can take one of the corporate lofts if you need to."

"Yes, sir," Kit said softly. "I just need to go home and pack a bag."

"Fine." The throbbing at his temples was threatening to choke the breath out of him. "I need some aspirin and coffee."

"Can I bring you some lunch?"

His stomach swooped and rumbled, but hunger was too small a part of it to chance food. "No. Just something for this headache."

He could feel her pause, her desire to do more. But he couldn't accept it. Couldn't let himself be weak right now.

"Thank you, Kit. Can you get legal on the phone?"

"Yes, sir."

She hadn't called him Henry in a week.

When she was gone, Henry let his body relax fully into the chair. He tilted it back, eyes closed.

He wanted to sleep.

The phone jarred him out of the drift he was falling into. With a sigh, Henry reached over and picked up.

ARCHIE MANAGED to keep the coffees from spilling, juggling two overnight bags and a tray of lattes as he walked down the hallway. Kit had sent him a pleading email an hour ago, begging for help with Henry. Another day, another tantrum. Another scene in the Jekyll and Hyde roller coaster they were enduring.

It's the concussion, said Evelyn.

It's the grief, said Libby.

It's the pressure, bitched Kit.

They all looked to him to handle it.

"Oh, thank you, thank you," Kit whimpered when he came into view. The young woman seemed to have aged a decade in the past seven days; even her bright red hair seemed duller.

"There's a bag of cookies in my suit pocket," he said, putting the tray on her desk. He dropped the bags on the visitor's chair as Kit made a dive for the refreshments. "Where's Henry?"

"Legal. Again. He practically lives up there. Or publicity." Kit sniffed the latte, then took a sip. Her face exploded into bliss. "I love you."

"Still gay, sorry." Archie settled into the other chair.

"I'm willing to pretend if you are," she teased.

"Ew," he shot back, and they both laughed.

A clearing throat turned their attention a second later.

Henry—frowning like he'd caught them doing something besides laughing—stood behind them.

"Am I interrupting something?"

The tone made Archie sit up. Kit nearly dropped her coffee in her lap.

"I brought some good caffeine. And cookies." He gestured to the bag and tray on Kit's desk. "Plus some things from home."

He kept his voice casual. Cool. Henry's expression didn't change.

"Well, break's over. Kit, I need you in the office." Henry walked past Archie, not giving him a second glance. Kit hurried after him, pen and notepad in hand.

When the door slammed behind them, Archie blinked in shock.

Chapter Twelve

"Good news," David said, walking into Henry's office unannounced.

Henry resisted the urge to throw the phone at his head.

"What?"

"I spoke to some board members—they seem to be responding to your campaign." He plopped himself in the visitor chair, clearly pleased.

"Thank God." Henry checked the time. Half past seven. He'd resolved to go back to the estate tonight. To eat a real meal and sleep a full night.

And see Archie.

The past seven days had been strained. Henry was an asshole; Archie retreated. Archie acted like an employee, Henry got more frantic. They were on the edge of implosion, it seemed, every hour of the day.

"Oh, and I did you a favor."

"A favor?"

"Archie Banks. I got him a job. A real one." David picked some lint off his sleeve.

Henry blinked at him. "What?"

"A job. My friend Charles, at Brighton Chemical? He needs someone in his international contracts department. I recommended Archie, and voilà—problem solved."

"Why was it a problem that Archie was working for me?" Henry asked slowly and deliberately.

David looked surprised. "He's got nothing but gossip and whispers surrounding him. It's all over the building that the FBI thinks he might be involved in the kidnapping."

"It's been almost a month. They have nothing—no proof. If they haven't arrested him...."

Henry shook his head. No, that wasn't what he wanted to say.

"He didn't do anything. He doesn't have to leave."

With that Henry grabbed his phone and stood up. "I'm going home," he announced, waiting for David to get the hint.

IN THE car, Henry was quiet, watching the back of Archie's neck with painful intensity. They were halfway home, cruising along the Thruway, when the words tumbled out of his mouth.

"Pull over somewhere private," he croaked.

Archie said nothing, but at the next exit, he put on his turn signal.

They ended up at a scenic overlook, empty in the darkness save for an 18-wheeler at the opposite end. Before Archie could put the car in park, Henry was undoing his tie, his jacket following a second later.

"Come back here, please." The begging note to his voice should cause him shame, but not this time.

Archie pushed the passenger seat all the way forward, squeezing himself into the back seat with amazing agility considering his injured leg. Henry pulled at Archie's belt; he licked his lips as Archie began to pull his jacket off.

He was naked first, panting and eager as Archie—still wearing his pants—yanked Henry over, pushing him onto his hands and knees with greedy hands.

"Please," was all Henry managed before he felt those big, hot hands kneading and pressing his ass open. He dropped his head, moaning, as Archie's tongue flicked over him roughly.

Henry pushed against the door, eyes screwed shut. Archie was relentless, using his tongue as a penetrating weapon. No casual kisses, no soft licks. Just ownership, demanding and angry as if punishing Henry with pleasure until he surrendered.

His dick was hanging heavy between his legs, but he didn't touch himself. Nails digging into the leather seat, tremors dancing up his spine. Shocks of arousal sparking from the wet tongue pushing into him.

A finger. Then two. There was no lube, nothing more than sweat and spit, but Archie didn't stop. Three fingers and the silence was chased away by Henry's moaning, which couldn't be contained another second.

It hurt so good, replacing the constant throb in his brain with a sharp knife, slicing him in two.

That fierce tongue circled and pressed between the thrusting fingers. Henry nearly cried as his orgasm stayed just out of his reach.

Archie wrapped his hand around Henry's cock, moved once, twice, and God, the blade cut him open and he was done, coming between the twin forces of Archie's hand and his mouth.

He collapsed on the seat, his entire body throbbing in time with his heart.

Archie cleaned him up. Dressed him. Handed him a bottle of water.

Wiped his face when he started to cry for no reason a few minutes later.

He was falling apart, into a million pieces.

"Shhh, go to sleep, baby," Archie whispered.

Henry closed his eyes and realized it was the only thing his lover said for the entire ride.

Chapter Thirteen

Archie waxed the BMW in the driveway, enjoying the steady beat of the sun on his back. It wasn't something he did often, but the chance to be outside and have some quiet time was too good to pass up.

Living in this house was starting to wear on him.

While it was the place he'd spent most of his childhood, it was different now—full of ghosts and anxiety, people trying to put their lives back together. So many broken things.

His mother was taking care of Libby now that Archie was back on his feet. It made her feel needed, and Libby certainly required some attention. The young widow had gone from stoic to insomniac to a weeping mess over the past few weeks. Evelyn felt tea and sunshine would improve her state; the doctors gave her antidepressants and sleeping pills.

Archie thought the answer lay somewhere between the two extremes.

Libby wasn't the only one on a downward spiral. Henry continued to grow angrier and more erratic as the days went by. With the board meeting only two weeks away, the stress was ratcheted up to "nuclear reactor meltdown."

Archie was tired, and not just physically.

After the bizarre sexual meltdown in the car, he and Henry hadn't been intimate. They'd barely spent any time together; during trips back and forth to the city, Henry slept. During the day, he was locked in his office with Kit and David.

David Silver.

Archie made a face at his reflection in the BMW's hood.

The man clearly couldn't stand him; it made Archie miss the days of indifference. One second he was offering Archie a job at a friend's company; when Archie demurred, his demeanor got nasty. He never missed an opportunity to throw out a comment about the investigation, the insinuation that Archie was suspect number one for the FBI.

His bank records were checked. His phone. His credit history. He'd endured two more interviews with the asshole Agent Feller.

He was completely innocent—why did he feel like they were going to show up with cuffs?

Sweating, Archie took a break. He sat on the decorative rock near the garage; he had a water bottle hidden in the shade, so he reached for that.

"Archie? Archie?" A frantic Hilary began to call him from the window behind him.

He jumped up, responding to the concern in her voice. "What's wrong?"

"It's Magnus; come quick."

EXHAUSTION AND old age, the doctor said, but in more diplomatic terms. Magnus had to take a break immediately—complete rest and attention from loved ones, far away from the demands of the estate.

With his protestations loud and unhappy, Magnus was shipped off to Florida to stay with his daughter.

Harold Magnus apparently had a first name *and* a daughter. It was all very shocking.

The security office from WalkCom sent over a slender young man named Carl, tall as an NBA player who didn't look strong enough to open a jar but proved helpful to Evelyn and Hilary by carrying groceries and running errands.

It was all they needed at this point. A butler was a relic of the old days, with parties and formal meals, neither of which happened anymore. The "staff" ate in the kitchen. Libby stayed in her rooms, still unsure as to what she wanted to do—and given free rein to live there as long as she wanted—and Henry lived in the study when he was even there.

Fractured. All of them.

Chapter Fourteen

Libby was lying on a delicate pink lounge, nearest the plank of sunlight coming through the farmost wall of the solarium. In a pair of black sweats and a gray yoga top, she looked oddly out of place in the ornate room.

"Hi, Archie," she murmured, turning her head to face him. Her paleness and quiet tone broke Archie's heart.

He went to her side quickly, helping her sit up.

"Thanks. Sorry—the doctor gave me this ridiculous sleeping pill, and I can't wake up." Libby swung her legs over, then patted the space next to her. "I'm thinking of skipping it tonight. I'd like to have my faculties back."

Archie sat gingerly, dwarfing her with his size. He felt awkward on this delicate bit of furniture. Mostly it felt strange to be sitting so close to Libby.

"I got your note, but I'm not sure why we have to be so… discreet… about talking."

Archie held his breath.

"I'm concerned about Henry, as I know you are. Of course it's expected after what happened, but the paranoia. It seems wildly over the top."

He let out a frustrated sigh. "Yeah. I know."

"This business with the board is overwhelming—I don't know that he's had the time to grieve." Libby sighed dramatically. "Everything makes him angry. He's not eating. Sleeping. Just poring over the books and every scrap of paper in Norman's office, all hours of the night."

Libby patted Archie's knee. "I was thinking we might come up with some ideas to help Henry."

"Whether he likes it or not?"

She shrugged one delicate shoulder. "Yes. I refuse to let him work himself to death. Norman wouldn't have wanted that."

"That's not the impression Henry had," Archie muttered, then stiffened in embarrassment. "Oh—Mrs. Walker, excuse me."

Libby put her hand up. "Archie, please call me Libby. And please don't apologize for speaking your mind. I loved Norman very much, but I'm not under any delusions regarding his parenting skills."

Or lack thereof. It hung in the air between them.

"Henry's always been concerned with living up to Norman's expectations." Archie slumped down. "And now he's never going to get the acknowledgment he's craved."

"Oh, Archie, I knew I chose the right person to talk to."

"I...."

"Norman was a difficult man—I'm not denying that. But he loved Henry so, so much. And I don't believe the will was meant to be a slam against Henry. I hate that he's taking it that way."

Libby looked up at him with sad eyes.

"I'm racked with guilt, Archie. I wish I had done a better job of convincing Norman to reach out a bit more to Henry when he was alive." She sniffled. "I miss him so much."

She started to cry, and Archie automatically reached out to draw her into his arms. He let her weep against his shoulder, awkwardly patting her back. He wished his mother were here, he wished....

And that was when he saw Henry, framed in the opening archway of the room.

The expression on his face—it was the same one Archie had seen when Henry had walked in on him and Kit talking that day in the office.

Jealousy.

Archie sighed, gently disentangling himself from Libby. "Henry's here," he murmured. Libby looked up in surprise, wiping at her eyes ineffectually.

Archie got up and walked toward Henry. He couldn't help noticing the dark circles under Henry's eyes, the grayish pallor to his skin. He was leaning against the wall, his tie askew.

"What the hell are you doing?" Henry asked, voice low and shaky.

Archie got closer. "Libby was upset."

"You told me you had a doctor's appointment in the city," Henry snapped. "You lied."

"Libby was upset and needed to speak with me," Archie said evenly.

"You're a fucking liar. What else have you lied about? Maybe the FBI was right about you! And you!" Henry turned his anger toward Libby, who stood behind Archie. "Why the hell are you still here?" His face got ugly with rage. "Trying to fuck your way to another rich husband?"

Libby gasped.

Archie watched him go from quietly annoyed to roaring fury in a few seconds, and the oddness of it, the sheer "not Henry" reaction, gave him pause.

"Calm down." It came out far gentler than Archie meant it to; he put his hand up in a supplicating gesture, and it was that motion that set Henry off.

He lunged at Archie, already off balance as he pushed away from the wall. There was a wheeling of arms, but Archie barely flinched as he caught Henry's body to his.

"Henry, stop, stop," Archie yelled as he grabbed Henry's arms, forcing him against the wall. He used his body as leverage to stop the crazed flailing.

The glassiness of Henry's eyes scared him more than the aborted attack.

"You want to fuck Libby? How about Kit? What the fuck is wrong with you?" Henry screamed, his voice breaking in the middle of his words, trickling off in a choked sound. Henry looked so confused, bucking his body against Archie's.

Like he didn't know why he was there.

"Shhhh," Archie murmured, feeling the fight go out of Henry. The brace of their bodies became less about control and more about comfort as Archie loosened his grip. "Easy there, love," he whispered as Henry's limbs went lax under his hands.

"Archie?" Henry said, blinking up at him. "I don't—"

"I know—let's go sit down, all right? You look a little pale." Understatement. Henry looked like the sky during a blizzard—a whiteout—the only color in his face the piercing blue of his eyes.

"Yes, all right." Henry let Archie manhandle him, leaning against him as he lost more and more of his ability to stand up. They barely made it to the lounge before he collapsed.

Libby pressed a blanket into Archie's hands before rushing past him and out the doorway. Archie didn't ask where she was going; his entire being was trained on Henry, who was sprawled on the lounger, breathing erratically.

"Archie?"

"Yes, relax." Archie tucked the blanket around Henry's body, smoothing it over him until the shaking slowed. His heart raced with fear. This wasn't anger or paranoia. Henry was ill.

Archie heard footsteps behind him; he didn't turn around, his focus lost in Henry's pale face and rapidly blinking eyes.

"I called an ambulance." It was Libby, her voice full of tears. "Your mother is back. And Carl. Do you want to move him or…."

"No, thank you. He'll be fine here." Archie stroked Henry's damp forehead, brushing away the hair from his eyes.

"They said ten minutes." Libby came to stand on the other side of the chaise, her hands clasped against her chest. "What could be wrong?"

"Maybe the concussion." Archie soothed Henry's eyes closed with gentle touches. "Maybe…." He didn't finish the sentence. The clatter of footsteps cut him off.

"My heavens," Evelyn breathed, the drag of her leg announcing her presence.

Archie felt his mother's hand against his shoulder.

"Mum, what does it remind you of?" he asked, looking up at her with hope in his voice—and a touch of desperation. Something wasn't right; he could feel it in his bones.

"Liquor?" she asked, frowning. "No—it's like… when he was a boy, he had a bad reaction to steroids." Evelyn's expression deepened. "Practically hallucinating."

"He hasn't been taking anything that I know of," Libby offered. "And he barely drinks water, let alone alcohol."

A cold chill settled under Archie's skin. He nodded.

"When we get to the hospital, you need to tell the doctors to check for steroids. And anything else that doesn't belong in his system," Archie said.

Libby gasped.

"God in heaven," Evelyn murmured, her hand tightening on Archie's shoulder.

"Just keep it quiet, okay? No one but the three of us and the doctors." The number of people Archie could trust was withering away to nothing. Below his hand, Henry had drifted off, an unnatural sleep as he moved restlessly.

Commotion caught all their attentions, and Libby hurried to direct the paramedics in.

"Mum?" Archie turned to face her.

"Yes, dear?"

"You're the last person I can trust entirely." His voice cracked. "We have to watch Henry carefully."

"It's not your fault, Archie." Evelyn touched his cheek lovingly. "Not at all. We'll protect him, I promise."

Archie nodded, his throat closed with fear.

The paramedics didn't take long to make it to the solarium. The young man and older woman were efficient and polite, even as they moved Archie away from Henry's still form.

"We think he might have had a bad reaction to one of the medications he's been taking," Libby said, her voice unnaturally loud.

"Thank you," the female paramedic said.

And then it was quiet as they took Henry's vitals and prepared him for transport.

Chapter Fifteen

Archie drove the BMW, following the ambulance as they headed toward the small local hospital. Libby sat beside him, her purse clutched in her lap, knuckles white against the strap. Evelyn sat in the back seat, the role reversal not lost on Archie in his haze of nerves.

"We need to keep an eye on who comes and goes," Archie said, tapping on the steering wheel. He lowered the heat so he could lower his voice. "Perhaps close the room to visitors if we can."

"God, Archie—do you really believe someone would do that?" Libby's voice quivered. "Drug Henry?"

"We still don't know who was behind the kidnapping, not really. And what someone would be willing to do to get control of the board."

They paused briefly at a stop sign before taking off again.

"This is just awful. Awful. I'm going to call the security company we're using on the grounds. They should send someone to the hospital. And—we need to call that FBI agent." Libby pulled her phone from her purse.

Archie nodded, relieved as he spied the hospital up ahead. He followed the directions to visitor parking, hands shaking as he retrieved the ticket from the automatic kiosk at the entrance of the lot.

He would protect Henry, no matter what it took.

At the front desk the trio was redirected to the emergency room. Henry had been whisked away behind the heavy swinging doors, and they couldn't go back, not yet at least.

Evelyn needed to sit down; Archie settled her and Libby in chairs close to the admitting desk so he could keep a watch for the doctors.

And then he paced.

"Should we call someone at the office?" Libby fretted to him on one of his passes.

"No." Archie looped around the chairs, down a small hallway to a soda machine, back through and down the hall to the bathrooms. Then back again.

"I wish they'd bloody hurry up," Evelyn bitched as he walked by.

Yes—he desperately wished that as well.

"Is Mr. Walker's family here?" A doctor was standing at the desk, looking around the semicrowded waiting room.

"We're here with Mr. Walker," Archie said, gesturing to Libby and Evelyn.

"I'm Mrs. Walker. His stepmother." Libby didn't even flinch at the man's dubious expression or the one he cast at Archie. "Archie and Evelyn are family."

The doctor clearly didn't care, though he might enjoy some salacious gossip if his expression was anything to go by. Archie suspected he had no idea who Henry was.

"I'm Dr. Bonner. Mr. Walker seems to be having an allergic reaction."

Archie felt his stomach twist into knots of fear. He hated being right about this.

"We've taken some blood to test." Dr. Bonner paused. "He says he isn't taking any medication right now. Is there a family doctor we can speak to, to confirm this?"

Libby and Archie exchanged looks; her nod was miniscule.

"Dr. Bonner, could we speak privately?" Archie lowered his voice. "I believe we need to contact an FBI agent, and things need to be kept quiet."

Dr. Bonner blinked in surprise. "Of course." He gestured them to follow him back into the emergency room.

"I'll stay here," Evelyn said, her hand tight on her cane.

Archie smiled and squeezed her arm. "All right, Mum. Could you call back to the house—let Hilary and Carl know what's going on? They shouldn't talk to anyone who comes to the house or calls. No word of where Henry is."

"Of course." Evelyn leaned up, and he met her halfway for a kiss to the cheek. "Sending Henry my love."

Archie gave her a reassuring nod and then turned to follow Libby and Dr. Bonner through the swinging doors. He had just a few moments to catch the doctor up on what exactly was going on.

HENRY WAS lying on a bed, tucked in a corner cubicle, hooked up to an IV and several monitoring devices. He'd been stripped down to his undershirt and slacks.

He looked slightly less like death, something that reassured Archie right now.

"Mr. Walker? I have your family here," Dr. Bonner was saying as Libby went to Henry's side. She took his hand in hers, squeezing gently.

Henry opened his eyes wearily, blinking under the bright overhead light.

His gaze immediately went to Archie, standing still as a statue at the bottom of the bed. Tears welled, and Archie put a reassuring hand on his ankle through the blanket.

"Sorry," he began, but Archie squeezed gently.

"You're sick. A bad reaction to something. Just relax," he said softly. Henry nodded and closed his eyes again.

"We're going to keep him until the test results come back. And you wanted to make a phone call," Dr. Bonner murmured, looking from Libby to Archie.

"I'll make the call." Libby leaned down and kissed Henry on the cheek. "Just rest, dear. I'll be back shortly."

Libby smiled at Dr. Bonner and briefly touched Archie's arm before leaving the cubicle.

"When I hear something from the lab, I'll be back," Dr. Bonner assured them. Henry's eyes were still closed, so Archie extended his hand.

"Thank you. We appreciate your help with this."

They shook, and Dr. Bonner departed a few seconds later, leaving Archie and Henry alone.

Archie found a visitor's chair in the corner and pulled it closer to sit next to Henry.

"I don't know what's wrong," Henry said so softly Archie almost missed it.

"I'm thinking someone gave you steroids—you're allergic. Do you remember that?" Archie's voice was hushed.

Henry's face contorted; his eyes opened as he turned his head to look at Archie. "When I was little."

"Right. You didn't take anything yourself, did you? No medications. No vitamins."

"No. Nothing." Henry licked his lips; then his confused expression grew panicked. "Someone gave me something."

"Yes."

"They're poisoning me." The fear in Henry's voice made Archie move; he stood up to lean over Henry's body, raising a soothing hand to touch his face.

"I promise I will make sure no one hurts you, Henry. I swear. But first, you have to believe it's not me. I could never hurt you—ever."

The impassioned words somehow penetrated the fog Henry was in; he shivered under Archie's gaze, nodding weakly.

"You would never hurt me."

"Never. It's my job to protect you—and I will." Archie didn't think about what happened next; it was natural and necessary to brush a kiss against Henry's clammy forehead, then against his dry lips.

"Sorry," Henry whispered, broken and sad.

"Don't apologize, please. You're sick, and we will talk when you're feeling better," Archie said firmly.

Henry listened, finally, breathing deeply as he curled closer to Archie.

And Archie worried that his lover could hear his heart pounding out of his chest.

They stayed like that, silent and tucked into each other, until Archie's back ached. But he couldn't move away.

LIBBY AND Dr. Bonner returned at approximately the same time; Archie heard them, straightening up with a quiet groan. At some point Henry had drifted off to sleep, and Archie didn't want to disturb him.

When he turned around, both of them were frowning.

"Let's speak out here," Dr. Bonner said quietly, beckoning Archie to follow.

"The FBI is on their way," Libby whispered as Archie came up next to her.

Archie nodded. "Good."

In the hallway, Dr. Bonner waited, his former cool and collected demeanor gone.

"What's wrong?" Archie asked.

Dr. Bonner took a deep breath. "You were correct. There is a huge amount of steroids in his system. More than a doctor would prescribe."

Archie swallowed hard. "How long before it wears off?"

"A few days. He should feel much better in an hour or so, but the muscle aches and weakness will continue for a while. The anger and paranoia should subside pretty quickly."

"He had a severe concussion recently. About four weeks ago."

"Ah—okay. Can you tell me where he was treated? I need to get his chart."

Libby already had her phone out. "This is the attending doctor. And our personal physician. He was the one checking on Henry after we brought him home."

She showed Dr. Bonner the numbers, and he quickly wrote them down on Henry's chart.

"Thank you. Let me give them both a call—we might need to run some additional tests." Dr. Bonner gave them each a nod and hurried away.

Archie felt his knees weaken.

"This is crazy," Libby murmured. "Crazy. What should we do, Archie? Call the security firm?"

"No—no one goes into the house unless we know we can trust them." Archie ran a hand over his face. "Which means we can't let Henry go back to the house until Carl is checked out and we get another security company."

"He was thoroughly investigated before—"

"By whom, Libby?" he broke in.

She stopped, nodded. "The security office at WalkCom."

"So we're not going home. We'll go to Mum's apartment. It's small, but we can manage. Less to check and maintain."

"Where should I go, then?"

"Home. We'll keep up appearances."

"And when they ask where Henry is?"

"Tell them he's staying at a hotel in the city to be closer to the office." Archie looked at his watch, in desperate need of coffee and food and peace. "Actually, Kit can start that going now. I'll have her leave the office early with a stack of folders and his laptop."

"You're very good at this spy stuff." Libby laughed weakly, her hand fluttering against her chest. "You missed your calling."

"Don't know about that. Still can't be sure who's doing this." Archie reached into his pocket for his phone. "I'm going to call Kit and talk to my mum."

Libby nodded. "I'll sit with Henry."

Archie watched her go into the cubicle and then headed back down the hallway and through the swinging doors. Everyone from the hospital personnel to the patients and their families received a long, hard look. Paranoia wouldn't serve him—he needed to think carefully about access and motive.

"Mum?" Archie dialed Kit's private cell number. His mother stood shakily as he approached. "I'm going to need a favor."

Kit picked up after the first ring. "Hello?"

Archie held up his hand to stay his mother's questions.

"Kit, it's Archie. I need you to do something for me."

By the time Archie and Kit finished their brief conversation, Evelyn was clearly bursting with questions.

And the FBI had arrived.

Agent Feller and his partner were standing a few feet away, waiting politely for Archie to get off the phone.

He heard their conversation in snippets. Then the younger agent said, "Inside knowledge and a big bankroll don't necessarily equal results. Or maybe money wasn't what they were after."

Archie lost track of everything for a second, then walked over.

"Agents," Archie said, reaching his hand out.

"Mr. Banks." Agent Feller smiled faintly. "We received a call from Mrs. Walker."

"The doctor has confirmed a large dose of medication that Henry has a bad reaction to in his system. It wasn't anything Henry took on his own." He let the words sink in.

The gray-suited agents shared identical looks.

"Can we speak to the doctor?"

"Dr. Bonner. I'll ask for him to be paged." Archie gave his mother a reassuring look before leading the agents to the front desk.

"We'll take it from here, Mr. Banks. Thank you." Agent Feller dismissed him, still with the polite smile.

"Fine. I'm going back to sit with Henry."

Agent Feller shook his head. "I don't think that's a good idea."

Archie had had enough.

"Unless you have evidence to prove I was involved in the kidnapping or have ever done anything to Henry, I will be sitting with my friend," he snapped, conscious of the people milling around, trying to see what was going on. "Why don't you do your fucking jobs and protect him?"

With that Archie walked back to his mother, the rage running over his skin like a rash.

"What is it?" Evelyn asked as he dropped down to a crouch so she wouldn't have to get up.

"Take a car back to your apartment. Please. Get it ready for Henry and me. I need somewhere safe to keep him." Archie's words ran out, that frantic fear bubbling up inside him again.

Evelyn nodded, her eyes wide and round.

"Of course, love. Right away."

"You don't tell anyone where you're going or what we're going to do."

Evelyn's mouth was a tight line; Archie hated worrying his mother, but he was running out of ideas.

"Yes," she murmured.

"Thank you," Archie said, grateful down to his soul. "Use Tommy's car service. Ask him to bill me later. No credit cards."

"All right." Evelyn cupped his face with both hands, her expression utterly serious. "You be careful, Archie. Don't be so worried about Henry that you forget to protect yourself."

"Promise," Archie whispered.

She kissed him on the forehead and let him go, already focused on her "assignment."

When Archie stood back up and turned around, the FBI agents were gone. He took that as further evidence they had jack shit on him. And no way to stop him from being with Henry.

Chapter Sixteen

Henry worked his way back to consciousness one tiny step at a time; when he could finally open his eyes, he was greeted by a reassuring sight.

Archie. Sitting at his bedside, chin dropped to his chest.

He started to ask why he was there when the aches hit him all at once. It felt like he had been pummeled. It felt like his head was going to split open.

It felt like the kidnapping.

Adding to his growing sense of dread, Henry couldn't remember what had happened.

"Archie?" he rasped, his mouth arid.

Archie's head popped up, his expression one of relief.

"Thank God." Archie was up in a flash, going to a small side table where a mustard-colored plastic pitcher waited. He poured a glass of water and returned to Henry's side.

"Drink this slowly, all right?" Archie's hand was strong and supporting under Henry's neck, making it easier to lift up and take a sip of the water.

It felt so good it nearly hurt.

He drank until the glass was empty, encouraged by the smile on Archie's face.

"There you go." Archie laid him back on the bed, and Henry sank into the pillows with relief.

"Where am I?"

"You don't remember?" Archie put the cup down on the side table, coming back to sit on the edge of the bed. "They admitted you to the hospital."

Henry frowned. His head ached, little bits of memory dancing around the throbs of pain.

"I…." The shame hit first, followed by the memory of attacking Archie—yelling and trying to hit him.

Archie's face softened. "You were sick, and you're sorry. We're not going to discuss this again," he said, stern and tender at once. "All I care about is you feeling better."

Conversations leaked back into his mind. "Steroids."

"Yes. They made you ill, and it worsened the symptoms of the concussion. They're keeping an eye on you, but you'll be fine."

"Who?"

Archie's expression changed into something tense. Worried.

"I don't know—but I will find out. Until I do, you're staying with me."

"I accused you of trying to sleep with Libby."

"And Kit," Archie said, with an attempt at levity.

"God."

Shrugging, Archie dropped his gaze to the blanket covering Henry's legs. "So you forgot I was gay—clearly I haven't been proving that to you enough lately."

Weakly, Henry reached to touch his lover, grasping his wrist and pulling it to his chest. "I love you," he whispered. He glanced at Archie's face, at the doubt and sadness playing over his beloved features. It hurt to see Archie like this, worse to know he was the cause.

Finally Archie looked at Henry, straight in the eye. "I love you too. And we'll talk about everything else when I know you're safe."

"Thank you," Henry murmured, not letting go of Archie's wrist.

They sat quietly for a while. The private room was darkened to relieve Henry's tired eyes and headache. Libby, he was told, had returned to the house to prepare a bag, and Evelyn was readying the apartment for his arrival.

"I'm going to your mother's place?" he asked, surprised. Henry assumed the fortresslike house was safer.

"Not many people know of it. And it's smaller—I can tell what's going on a bit better than in that fifteen-bathroom monolith," Archie said gently, teasing him.

"That's a good plan, actually."

Archie played with the corner of the blanket, smiling. "Thank you. Libby thinks I missed my calling as a spy."

"She might be right. You do look amazing in a black suit." Henry felt his emotions bubbling up, right under the surface. He was sure there was a billboard across his forehead, broadcasting every feeling he had.

"Ah well—no uniform for now." Archie's warm, golden skin pinked around his cheeks. "Jeans. Sorry."

"I'll suffer," he murmured.

Archie looked at him then, right through him, it felt like, and Henry closed his eyes to stop the onslaught of things he wanted to say just watching his lover's face.

Henry swallowed. He heard Archie sigh loudly.

"You know I have no defense when you act all woebegone," he said.

Opening one eye, Henry tried to glare. "I'm not."

Archie regarded him, tilting his head left, then right. "Yes, you are. But I'm letting it slide since you're sick."

"Not sick, poisoned." Henry opened both his eyes. "And scared shitless."

"We'll figure this out. I promise."

"The FBI…."

"Is still sniffing around." Archie shook his head, pressed the heel of his hand against his right eye. "I'm surprised Feller and his sidekick aren't in here, warning you to stay away from me."

"If they were before, I don't remember." Henry licked his lips. "Doesn't matter anyway. I don't believe them."

"Good."

Before he could say anything else, there was a gentle knock at the door. Dr. Bonner stuck his head in a second later.

"Mr. Walker, Mr. Banks." He entered the room, holding on to a file. "I'm glad I caught you awake. How are you feeling?"

"Run over by a truck several times." Henry looked at Archie, then at the doctor, who joined Archie at his bedside. "And a bit concerned with how little I remember from today."

"Well, your reaction to the medication is only partially to blame. The rest lies in the consequences of your concussion. I think you went back to work entirely too soon," Dr. Bonner said sternly. "You need to take it easy, and by that I mean bed rest and calm for a few weeks."

Henry scowled, shifting in the uncomfortable bed. "I have a business to run."

"Then run it from bed. Part-time. Delegate." The physician clearly wasn't interested in excuses. "Or else you'll be finding yourself back in here and facing some pretty serious consequences in not allowing yourself to heal."

Archie's stern face was equally matched by Dr. Bonner's, and Henry closed his eyes in annoyance.

"Fine," he said finally. "I'll take some time off, work from home." He opened his eyes. "Do a little less." Part of him was scared enough to take a break—but the other part knew WalkCom was in far too much turmoil and danger to turn things over to anyone else.

The only person he trusted implicitly at this point was Archie.

"I promise," he added, noting that Dr. Bonner seemed to have an advanced bullshit detector.

"I'll be with him at all times," Archie cut in, folding his hands together. He was using the chauffeur voice. "So I'll be able to manage his sleep schedule."

"Yes, he'll be happy to smother me with a pillow when I won't stop working," Henry said drily.

That finally satisfied Dr. Bonner.

"All right. Then I'll let you leave in a few hours, after you've had another IV of fluids. You're on the verge of dehydration, Mr. Walker. Mr. Banks is going to also have to manage your eating and drinking, clearly."

Dr. Bonner gave them both a smile and a nod, then headed out.

Henry tipped his head back and stared at the ceiling. "Stop enjoying this so loudly."

"I'm never going to enjoy seeing you in a hospital bed." Archie's sharp tone made Henry wince; he turned his head to look at his lover. Friend. Employee.

Everything.

"I know," he said gently. "I mean—bossing me around."

"I'd rather you could fight back." Archie's gaze dropped to the floor. "Will you be okay by yourself for about fifteen minutes? I want to make a few more follow-up calls and get everything set up."

"Of course." Henry pulled the covers a little higher.

"Fifteen minutes, no more. If anyone comes in here you don't know...." Archie reached into his pocket and pulled out his pager, the backup for his cell phone.

"Old school," Henry murmured as Archie put it into his hand.

"Keep it out of sight and send me a 911 page. I'll be right outside."

"Got it." Henry didn't tease the serious expression or spy-like request. He was scared enough to tuck the pager under the blanket, tight in his hand. "It'll be fine, though," he added to reassure them both.

"Fifteen minutes," Archie said again, reaching down to squeeze Henry's shoulder before stepping away.

"I'll be here."

Their gazes held long enough for Henry's heart to start beating wildly. The stormy blue of Archie's eyes made him dizzier than the concussion but made him feel far safer.

Without another word Archie turned and headed out the door.

Chapter Seventeen

Evelyn lived in the basement of a nineteenth-century row house in Prospect Heights on a tree-lined street. She had started renting years ago, a place she and Archie could have away from the estate, for vacations and weekends away. And the landlord treated her like family.

So when she called to say her son and his friend were staying there for a few days while she was away, Boris couldn't do enough. He met the cab, embracing Archie as soon as he stepped out onto the street.

"Archie!" The man came up to Archie's breastbone and patted his back with an enthusiasm that threatened to leave bruises.

"Hello, Mr. Akulov," Archie said, giving the man a one-armed hug in return. "You didn't have to meet us out here—we have the key."

"Your mother says to make sure you get inside with your friend. I make sure you get inside with your friend," Boris admonished. He twisted to look behind him and into the cab, where Henry waited patiently.

"Thank you." Archie untangled himself. "Come on, it's clear," he murmured to his lover, holding the door open and extending his hand.

"How very James Bond," Henry said as he slid out gingerly. He was still in pain, that much was clear to Archie, but he refused to admit it.

Archie gripped Henry's arm as he stood up, holding him steady. He helped him around the door, slamming it once he was clear, and led Henry to the sidewalk where a curious Boris was waiting.

"Hello, sir," Henry said politely to the wizened little man.

"Hello." Boris squinted. "You're the man who got kidnapped," he said bluntly.

Henry nodded even as Archie stiffened beside him. "Let's get inside," Archie said. He didn't want to be on the street in the open, didn't want Mr. Akulov to ask embarrassing questions.

The landlord let them pass but followed close behind as they made their way to the little iron gate that led to the door tucked behind the front stairs.

Archie unlocked the door and gently pushed Henry inside, conscious of their vulnerability. He turned around and gave Boris a serious stare.

"No one can know we're here, okay? We don't want the press bugging us," he said clearly and carefully.

Boris looked annoyed. "I know that. Your mother told me." He pursed his lips, clearly offended by Archie's assumption that he might have a wagging tongue. "I have lunch. I will bring down." He scowled, irritated but still hospitable.

Archie sighed, rubbed his forehead with the palm of his hand. "I'm sorry. It's just been very stressful lately."

"Of course." Boris Akulov straightened and nodded to Archie. "I will leave the lunch at the back door. You call me if you need more."

"Thank you, sir."

The landlord muttered something under his breath and left with a stomp, letting the gate slam behind him.

Archie was most definitely going to have to buy him an apology present.

He went into the apartment, locked the door—including the deadbolt—and pocketed the key. Henry had already turned on the lights, and the impact of being "home"—or the closest thing that wasn't the servant's apartment he'd had growing up—knocked the wind out of him.

He was tired. He was drained. He wished his mother was about to come out of the kitchen and announce stew and bread were on the table.

Archie's eyes burned. The scent of lemon verbena and steam from the pipes filled his senses and triggered so many memories.

"Archie? Are you all right?" Henry's voice cut through his exhaustion, and Archie pushed off the door to find his lover in the apartment.

It was a small place, beginning with the slightly cramped front room where Evelyn had her couch, easy chair, and television in a neat circle. Knickknacks were arranged with well-worn paperbacks in clean lines on the bookshelves.

In the next room was the kitchen—small but full of great smells lingering in the corners. It was spotless—because Evelyn Banks didn't tolerate a mess in the kitchen—with a tiny wood table tucked in the corner. It was covered with a lace doily, a red clay bowl full of apples in the center.

Henry wasn't there either. There were two more doorways—one to his right, one to his left. The right led to his mother's bedroom and the bathroom, the other to his old bedroom. He guessed where Henry was.

"In here," Henry called, confirming his guess. Through the doorway and into a morass of memories; Henry was sitting on the double bed, leaning against the iron headboard. Archie stood there, watching him, and marveled that there was enough oxygen in this closet of a room for both of them.

"You're too tall for here," Henry said, smiling wanly. He'd lost his jacket and shoes, sitting on the chenille bedspread in his black trousers and tight gray polo.

It was as if Archie's teenaged fantasies had come to life.

"I still sleep here sometimes, when I'm visiting Mum," Archie said. The walls were kelly green, the ancient wood floors battered by years of sports shoes and the wheels of Matchbox cars. Without a window, the only light was thrown by a lamp on the chest of drawers, a flea-market find better suited to a grandmother's parlor.

"Where are the posters of sweaty athletes and muscle cars?" Henry teased gently. He toyed with the nubby surface of the bedspread, tracing the faded blue circles.

"Mum didn't allow them—bad influences on a young mind." He laughed, undoing his jacket, then taking it off. He draped it over the hook on the door.

"I'm not surprised. That was the same reason she gave me." Henry looked at him, a critical expression on his face. "You're exhausted. Come lie down."

"I'm fine."

"You're exhausted." Henry slid over to the side of the bed flush against the wall.

"I should check the back door." Archie gestured, trying to remember his resolve that he was protecting Henry and nothing else.

"Your virtue is safe with me, Banks—I couldn't get it up if I tried," Henry said drily. He lay down on his back, sighing as he sank into the overly soft mattress.

"That isn't…." With a rumble of annoyance—he hated when Henry read his mind—Archie kicked off his shoes. He took a few steps to the bed and contemplated how stupid this was before sitting down on the edge.

"Are you cold?" he asked gruffly, and Henry laughed.

"Yes."

Archie reached under the bed until he felt the heavy quilt his mother kept there.

He took his time, unfolding the handmade quilt until he could drape it over his legs before lying flat next to Henry. Then he shared the blanket.

"See? Perfectly innocent." Henry's voice sounded sleepy, and he rolled over to press against Archie.

"Hush. Just a quick nap and then we'll…."

"Commence hiding out? Do we need to do something special?"

Archie twisted around a tiny bit, enough to find the groove he'd long established as the way to get comfortable in this bed. His ankles hung off the end, feet pressing up against the wall.

Henry didn't belong there, at least in theory. This—his mother and his little home away from the estate—was not anywhere Archie expected him to be, particularly curled up against his shoulder, breathing deeply in his ear.

"No, nothing special," Archie said quietly. He resisted the urge to touch Henry—right up until he took Henry's hand into his under the musty quilt. "Kit's going to bring work over so you can keep track of what's going on. But we'll limit how much time you have with anyone we don't trust."

"Which is?"

Archie laughed mirthlessly. "Everyone but you, me, and my mother."

"What about Kit and Libby?"

"Slightly more trusted than anyone else, but still, Henry—we have to be careful. There's someone on the inside."

The thought sent them both into silence; Henry tucked himself a bit closer, his chin on Archie's shoulder. He squeezed their fingers together, and Archie bit the inside of his cheek to keep quiet.

I love you. I've loved you since I was a child, and I will do anything to protect you. It was utterly terrifying to contemplate the depth of his feeling for Henry, the lengths he was willing to go to….

"Thank you, Archie," Henry said suddenly, his voice quiet and serious. "I don't know what I would do without you."

The silence was epic—loud and dramatic. Archie didn't possess the words to answer, so he just made a hushing sound.

"Go to sleep," he murmured, eyes already closed.

Chapter Eighteen

When Henry woke up, the room was pitch-black, the bed empty, and something smelled like a five-star restaurant had opened up in the next room.

The quilt was heavy on Henry's body, and it took him a few attempts to weakly shove it away. He inwardly cursed his current state; his head swam as he sat up, and his limbs sluggishly rearranged themselves into a position he could push up from.

Henry swung his legs over the side of the bed, breathing deeply. The sizzle and scent of bacon were clearly identifiable, along with coffee and the yeasty aroma of bread. For a second he let himself script a time when he wasn't hiding from someone trying to hurt him and destroy his father's company. When he could walk into the next room and put his arms around Archie, share a life when they were on equal footing—instead of Henry always feeling like each word, each action just wasn't good enough.

It only lasted a second, though; if he spent too long imagining that fantasy, it made his chest hurt.

Willing himself to steadiness, Henry stood up, balancing himself before taking a step. He tried to remember how many steps it took to get to the door, tentative as he walked in the darkness, one hand extended in front of him.

Nothing impeded him; he found the knob and gave it a twist, a squeak and a moan accompanying the motion of opening the door.

The light from the kitchen made him wince, one hand up to cover his eyes.

"Oh, sorry," Archie said, coming into view as Henry lowered his hand and blinked at his lover from the arch. "Wanted to make sure I didn't disturb you," he added. He stood at the stove, a dish towel over his shoulder, as he tended to a frying pan of bacon.

"It's fine." Henry looked at the set table, then to the windows. It was night. "How long did I sleep?"

"Five hours. I slept about four." Archie's expression was a bit sheepish as he turned back to the sizzle and snap of the food.

"Good." Henry slid into one of the padded chairs at the table, folding his hands on top. "You needed it. We both did."

"Been a hell of a few days. Weeks." Archie turned off the heat under the frying pan. "Months."

Henry grunted a response. "Maybe it'll be over soon. We'll go on vacation. A real one." His mouth kept going even as his brain sent him painful reminders of just how badly he'd treated Archie for so long. "Hawaii."

"We'll see," was all Archie said. Then there were only the sounds of the meal preparations being completed.

There was a plate of bacon, sliced tomatoes, hunks of Dublin cheddar, and a loaf of warmed bread from the oven. Henry's mouth watered as each plate appeared on the table, Archie returning a last time with a pot of coffee.

"Evelyn will be impressed when I tell her about your culinary skills," Henry said softly.

"I'm not sure this even counts as cooking." Archie poured them each a mug of coffee as Henry began to fill two plates with healthy portions of food. "Mmmm, we need mayo."

Henry made a face. "No, we really don't."

"Yes, we do." Archie was up again, back to the fridge.

"Actually butter might be nice," Henry called to him. The domestic warmth of the kitchen, the food—the fact that he felt well rested for the first time in months—cracked open something deep inside him. Something that tasted like relief and comfort, and Archie's grin as he rejoined Henry at the table.

With mayo and butter.

He cut them thick slices of the bread as Henry picked at bits of bacon on the serving plate. He tried to remember he was hiding, that he should be afraid.

Except he wasn't when he was with Archie.

"I am taking you away when this is done," Henry said boldly as Archie dropped two pieces of bread on his plate. He kept talking when he felt Archie tensing up. "I have a lot to make up to you, Archie."

Archie's gaze had fallen to his plate. "Henry—you don't have to...."

"Yes, I do." Henry pushed his way into Archie's refusal. "I care about you. So much. And yet, in the middle of realizing you are the only person in the world I trust, I pushed you away. And that is unforgivable."

"No, it's entirely forgivable," Archie said gently, lifting his face to smile sadly in Henry's direction. "You've had a lot going on, and we've never—we've never put a label on... this."

"Then that was a mistake." Henry reached across the table to take Archie's hand. "Before this all went to hell, I should have said—I should have said what I wanted to."

That must've gotten Archie's attention, because he shifted, shoulders raised; Henry held on to his hand that much harder.

"I wanted to say—Archie, I'm... I've been crazy about you since I was thirteen years old. It wasn't just about sex." His voice dropped to a whisper, the ache in his chest becoming deeper. "Don't leave. I don't want this to end."

"Henry, this isn't the time." Archie's voice was shot, like he'd been shouting for hours. Around them time seemed to stop—all sounds and smells of the kitchen disappeared.

"No, it's not. I should have said these things earlier, so you wouldn't think it's the grief talking." Henry pushed his chair closer, the screech of the legs against the linoleum deafening. "Please believe me. Of all the regrets I have, it's second only to hiding from my father."

Archie moved then, closing the distance between them to grasp Henry's face with both hands. "Stop," he murmured. "Just...."

"No—sorry. I love you and have for fucking years, and you're going to listen to me."

Archie's expression was one of warring emotions. Henry could read each one perfectly—the fear, the anger, the disbelief. The desperate hope that Henry was telling the truth.

"I love you," Henry repeated.

"Shut up." And then Archie kissed him like it was their last moment on earth.

ARCHIE DIDN'T want to argue anymore—he wanted to forget everything but the slick curve of Henry's tongue in his mouth and the hard planes of Henry's body under his hands. Twisting in the chair, he drew Henry closer, jolting the table and rattling everything as the close quarters blocked any further contact.

Henry pulled away, resting his forehead against Archie's jaw. "Bedroom?" he murmured, as breathless as Archie felt.

"Yes." Archie pushed his chair back and stood, taking Henry with him. He was still mindful of Henry's time in the hospital, the stress of the past weeks; Archie kept his lover close, hip to hip as they navigated their way to the bedroom.

A tiny, logical part of his brain insisted this wasn't a good idea, but when Henry stopped just inside the doorway to gently touch his face, all protestation ended.

"I love you," Archie blurted out, glad for the dark room, glad that Henry just laughed and stroked his fingers against the curve of Archie's face.

"You've said that." Henry leaned closer, warm and solid in Archie's embrace.

"For a long time." Archie felt idiotic, blurting things out like his filter had completely evaporated. "Since...."

"Since puberty?" Henry laughed, ducking his head.

"Is that a confession?"

"Yes."

The conversation ended again as hands slid down Henry's back, gripping his hips to pull Henry closer. Henry let out a soft sound, then brushed his lips over Archie's—a tease, a little taste of his desire.

Archie turned them, never letting go of Henry's body. He walked his lover backward the two steps to the bed.

"Let me," he whispered, moving to undo the buttons of Henry's shirt. The weak light from the kitchen kept Henry in the shadows, revealing tiny slivers of pale skin as Archie made quick work of each piece. The shirt, his jeans—each fell to the ground until Henry stood before him in just his boxers.

Henry let out a little shiver; whether it was from the dark room or desire, Archie couldn't be sure, but it kicked his protective instincts into high gear. "Under the covers." He slid his arm around Henry's waist, relishing the touch of their bodies before easing him back onto the bed.

"Only if you come with me," Henry said, his hands pulling Archie down to the mattress with him.

"Need to get undressed."

"I can help with that."

"Mmmm."

Henry cut off Archie's words with a well-timed kiss, catching him as he bent to grab the quilt. His hands moved just as quickly, grabbing the bottom of Archie's T-shirt to pull it over his head.

"Too long," Henry muttered as they broke apart; their hands worked together to lift his shirt off. Archie felt Henry's increasingly frantic hands on the elastic waist of his sweatpants.

They stripped the last bits of clothing, tossing them to the ground. It was a tangle of limbs as they fell onto the bed, Henry on top of Archie.

"I've missed you," Henry whispered, pressing kisses between the words against Archie's jaw.

"I've always been here." Archie ran his hands up Henry's back, worshipping each muscle and the expanse of skin with his touch.

They kissed, long and deep, tongues plunging to explore, getting twisted in the middle. Henry rubbed against Archie, working their bodies together with a purpose. Archie rutted up, wanting to move, to roll them over, to....

"Let me," Henry moaned against his jaw. "Just... let me."

To give up the control wasn't easy, but Archie nodded, pressing back into the mattress as Henry moved above him. He sank into the bed under the attention of Henry's mouth, as he roamed over Archie's chest with purpose. Sucking one nipple, then the other, nipping at the freckles on his shoulder. Groaning, Archie let his hands fall to his sides, gripping the sheets and blankets below him.

Henry moved again, his hips never stopping their rhythm as he sat up. He licked his palm twice, the slick sound of tongue to skin making Archie's back arch.

"Fuck," Henry whispered, taking both their cocks in his dampened hand, rocking forward and back… slowly. "Just like this."

"Oh God."

Archie let the smooth glide of skin on skin lull him. He let himself be taken under by Henry's touch and scent.

The bed rocked beneath them; sweat slicked where their bodies met. Henry pushed up on his knees, angling each thrust downward now, and Archie gasped at the sensation.

They kissed.

Archie was so caught up in the sensation, he was unprepared for Henry coming first, spilling warm stripes of come over the head of his cock. Henry never stopped, never missed a stroke—the come made it wetter and slicker, and Archie shook with the force of his own release when he followed a few seconds later.

The mess didn't matter. Breathless, Archie pulled Henry down so they were chest to chest, mouths crashing together in a lush kiss.

When Henry pulled away, he didn't go far. He traced Archie's bottom lip with his tongue, eyes bright and focused for the first time in a long time.

"How long before you can fuck me?" he whispered hotly.

Archie's cock twitched as he tangled one hand in Henry's hair, locked in place as he plundered his lover's mouth.

Not soon enough.

Chapter Nineteen

THE NEXT morning—late in the morning, since they didn't actually settle down to sleep until four, having returned to their forgotten meal for some postcoital snacking—Henry cooked breakfast.

Oatmeal and bacon and tea, but it was edible, and that was an accomplishment.

Archie stripped the bed, then showered, joining Henry at the table with damp hair and dressed in only sweatpants.

Henry tried not to stare.

"What do we do today?" Henry asked, pulling his chair a bit closer to Archie's.

"Kit should be dropping off some work, plus your laptop. I'm thinking of taking a nap." He dropped a kiss on Henry's cheek, then stole his bacon.

"Don't you have spy things to do?"

It was lighthearted, but Archie didn't smile.

"I'm working on keeping you safe. That's all." There was schoolwork and finals, but he just couldn't think of those things right now. Not when Henry wasn't safe.

"But if we could figure out who it is…."

Archie nodded. "Who has the most to gain from you not being the president and CEO?"

"Definitely someone on the board."

"How well do you know them?"

"Some have been around as long as David and my father. Others are unknowns, really. I know them superficially."

Archie didn't speak for a few minutes.

"Maybe we should hire a private investigator. Someone who reports to only us," Henry offered.

"That's a good idea, actually."

"Thank you for sounding surprised." Henry turned his attention to his breakfast—and stole back his bacon.

KIT STOPPED by a few hours later with the promised work and laptop. She and Henry sat in the living room, but not before Henry offered her a complete explanation of what the doctor had told him. The steroids, the poisoning.

"So I'm sorry. I treated you horribly, and I apologize," Henry said sincerely, reaching over to pat her hand.

Kit blew out a breath. "Wow. God—that sucks. Do you feel okay now?"

"A lot better. We're assuming I was being fed a dose every day; that's why I was…."

"Such an asshole?" Archie called from the kitchen.

Hand over her mouth, Kit snickered.

"We should probably get to work," Henry said loudly.

ARCHIE LET them go for four hours, offering tea and cookies halfway through.

The rest of the time he sat in the kitchen, doodling on a piece of paper. A timeline of the past few weeks.

Between the kidnapping and Henry's collapse.

Major events, people who were at the house.

His list of suspects were: Carl; the doctor who had been treating everyone in the house, and Paul, the driver, though the latter was a long shot. He'd been around longer than Hilary, and, though a quiet man, Archie had never had a moment of suspicion about him.

"Archie?"

He looked up; Henry was watching him from the doorway.

"How are you guys doing?"

"Done for the day, I think. Kit's going back to the office for an hour to make some copies."

Archie turned the pad over.

"How about dinner?"

"How about bed first?" Henry gave him a flirty little smile.

The bed was too small, but they made do; Archie curled around Henry, their legs scissored as Archie fucked him gently. Archie buried his face in the sweaty curve of Henry's neck, breathing in his musky scent. At every broken sound Henry made, Archie bit into his shoulder.

"You feel so good," Archie whispered, rubbing his hand down Henry's chest. "Every night I want to do this. Every night."

Henry got wild in his arms, shoving back to get more—more of Archie, more of the sensation, but Archie couldn't be rushed. He slowed the pace, keeping every stroke shallow until Henry started to beg.

"Come on, come on," Henry bitched at him.

Archie rocked, then stopped.

Henry vibrated. Clenched down hard on Archie's cock in retaliation.

"Bastard," Archie choked out. His free hand went to Henry's hip, keeping him in place as he started to move again.

HENRY ORDERED a pizza while Archie took another shower.

He sat at the table to wait—when he saw the pad, he flipped it over, curious as to what Archie had been doodling for so long that afternoon.

The timeline. The list.

Archie trying to solve this puzzle.

Henry picked up the pencil and traced over Archie's looping scrawl.

The kidnapping.

The reading of the will.

Henry goes back to the office.

Magnus leaves.

Henry's health starts to fail.

Henry collapses.

The list—Paul; the doctor, and Carl—barely made sense. Paul and Dr. Katz had been around for years. Carl was a kid who had been thoroughly vetted by their security department. What vendetta could he have against the family?

The doorbell rang while he was doodling.

"I got it." Archie darted through the living room before Henry could get to the front door.

Overprotective, Henry thought.

He didn't mind.

Chapter Twenty

Breakfast.
>Kit over with work.
>Lunch with Kit.
>Dinner.
>Sex.
>Television.
>Sex.

Five days of a routine that Archie wanted to keep up forever.

If only it wasn't for a terrible reason.

Henry finally looked like Henry again; bright eyes and clear skin, awake and alert. The specter was gone.

The list teased him.

At one point he wrote Libby's name and then quickly erased it. What did she have to gain? Would she have gotten more if Henry wasn't in the picture anymore?

The board meeting was in two days; if Henry was voted in as president and CEO, would this escalate?

Slowing him down was one thing.

Was killing him the next?

"Seriously, come and join us. You're looking all dour in here." Kit breezed into the kitchen, going straight for the fridge.

"Make yourself at home," he said drily.

"Thank you. My boss sent me in for waters and to tell you to come inside the living room."

"Yes, ma'am." He got up, flipping the pad over again.

In the living room, Henry was in the side chair, clicking away on the laptop and working as quickly as he could before Archie made him take a break. He'd fight the limited screen time on principle, but there was no denying the aftereffects of the concussion still lingered. His brow was furrowed as he scanned the document.

"You rang?"

Henry looked up with a start, but his face quickly melted into a smile.

Archie tried not to blush.

"I feel bad relegating you to the kitchen. Why don't you watch television or something?"

"Don't want to disturb you guys. And you know you're not supposed to be watching television anyway. Doctors orders."

Kit returned with two waters and a box of cheese crackers, dropping back onto the couch.

"Read a magazine." Henry's expression switched to imploring. "Come on."

Archie pretended to cave. "Fiiine. I'll read a knitting magazine and bask in your corporate glow."

"Ha. Watch it. When you start working in the world of international finance, you'll see. This is the glamour right here." Kit fiddled with the lid of the water.

Archie settled onto the opposite end of the couch, magazine in hand. He avoided eye contact with Henry, putting his feet on the ottoman. "You make a compelling case for retail."

They settled into relative silence. Kit on her laptop, Henry leaning over as they occasionally exchanging ideas or comments. Archie read about perfecting sock knitting, then drifted off for a nap not long after.

He dreamed about socks.

Then he dreamed about the kidnapping.

"Archie, wake up." Henry was shaking him, pulling him out of that terrifying moment of being on the ground when he woke up alone.

He sat up with a start, blinking the memories out of his eyes.

"It's okay; you're okay."

He looked into Henry's eyes and took a deep breath. "Yeah. Sorry."

Henry didn't ask what Archie had been dreaming about; from his expression, he didn't have to.

"Where's Kit?"

"She left about twenty minutes ago. I ordered Turkish food for dinner." Henry smoothed Archie's forehead. "You want to wash up?"

Archie couldn't help but smile. "You're strangely good at being domestic."

"I learned from your mom, the best of the best."

"You should tell her that; she'll love it." Archie pulled Henry onto the couch.

"Do you think…." Henry stopped, then started again. "Do you think she'd be happy if she knew about us?"

Us—that sounded lovely.

"She'd explode from sheer joy," Archie said, wrapping his arm around Henry's shoulders. "Then we'd both get in trouble for not telling her sooner."

Henry was quiet for a few minutes after that, rubbing his palm against Archie's knee. "I wonder what would have happened if I'd told my father."

"He might have surprised you." Archie shifted, laying his head on Henry's shoulder. "You never know."

"No," Henry agreed sadly. "I won't ever know."

THE FINAL proposals went out to all the board members. They would cast their ballots tomorrow, and Henry's fate would be known. The lawyers were preparing documents to contest the will if the vote went against him; it was a last-resort plan as far as Henry was concerned. To contest the will meant a hold being placed on all the other bequests, and he didn't want anyone to suffer.

They were alone by early afternoon; Henry sent Kit home for a well-deserved break. And he wanted a few minutes to enjoy the quiet with Archie before they were tossed back into stormy waters.

"Things are so up in the air. I feel like I can't make plans," Henry confessed as they lay in bed, Archie spooning Henry under the quilt. "And I'm sorry for that."

"I understand. Some things are beyond your control."

"They weren't beyond my control before, Archie—you can stop defending me." Henry turned his head to look Archie in the eye. "I don't need it, not about this."

"Fine. You didn't act; I didn't insist on it. Now we're sort of—dealing with things as they come."

"But together. We're dealing with it together." That was the only important part as far as Henry was concerned. He refused to sacrifice having Archie in his life.

"Right."

The lack of surety in both their voices lingered in the dark.

"I love you," Henry said again, as if repeating it would make everything all right.

Chapter Twenty-One

Henry sat in his usual spot at the enormous table they used for board meetings, almost twenty minutes early. He touched the leather portfolio in front of him, then rearranged his water glass and pen. The sun was streaming through the floor-to-ceiling windows, warming his face.

He felt clearheaded and healthy for the first time in weeks.

He felt absolutely sure what he wanted the outcome of today to be.

"You're early," a voice said behind him.

Henry turned to find David standing in the doorway, a slightly disapproving look on his face.

"Do I seem overeager?" Henry asked with a chuckle. He turned back around.

"Yes." Definite disapproval.

David took his place directly across from Henry, setting his briefcase on the floor by his feet.

"I've talked informally to a few board members, Henry. It's going to be close."

The stern tone of his godfather's voice made Henry a little concerned, but he just smiled. "It doesn't have to be a landslide—I just need the majority."

"Hmmm."

The conversation ended, and Henry stared down at the glass table. David didn't believe he had the votes to be elected. That was a tough one, but then again, he'd survived his father's lack of confidence. He could manage David's.

The room filled with board members, some greeting Henry warmly, others keeping their distance. A quick head count—clearly friendly, clearly distant, those he couldn't read—had it going either way.

It would be close.

"Good morning, everyone." Mr. Harvey walked to the head of the table, looking like a cheerful, beardless Santa. But instead of handing out candy, he had a folder with tallies of the vote.

And WalkCom's future.

Henry exhaled but continued his attempt to look completely calm about the outcome. They had to see his confidence.

He checked his watch.

Took a sip of water.

Mr. Harvey gave a brief speech about protocols, then opened his briefcase with a series of little snicks.

"Having totaled the votes, including proxies, the chairman and CEO of WalkCom will be…."

The pause was dramatic. Henry looked at a tiny sunbeam hitting the window above David's head.

"…. Henry Walker."

The room broke into applause, and Henry's entire body seized up with—joy. He was standing before it registered, having his hand shaken vigorously by Mr. Harvey.

Quickly he was surrounded by the board. He wanted to know the vote, wanted to know how many of the congratulatory backslaps and handshakes were real and how many were bred of disappointment and the covering of one's ass.

"We knew you could do it," someone said.

"Your father would be delighted," Xander Pense interjected, surprising Henry with a cool smile.

"It's an honor," a third chimed in.

Henry just nodded and accepted it all with grace and a steely determination in his eyes.

When the crowd eventually parted—because an assistant rolled a cart of champagne into the room—Henry noticed that David Silver was nowhere to be found.

ARCHIE WAITED in the executive office with Kit while the board meeting was going on. They didn't bother with conversation—both were too tense for that.

The Heir Apparent

When the phone buzzed, Kit almost fell out of her seat. She pressed the speaker button.

"Shelby?"

The assistant whispered into her phone. "I just brought them champagne. Henry was voted in."

Kit let out a wild whoop.

"Oh God, I have to go." Shelby hung up quickly as Kit twirled in her chair.

"My boss is the boss of everything," she chirped, giving Archie a giddy smile. "Yours too."

"Yeah, he is." Archie tried to organize his feelings. He was so proud of Henry—so proud of him convincing the board he was the right person for the job. But he was melancholy because the Henry he knew—and loved—was gone now. All those lovely plans in the hidden corner of his mother's apartment were just dreams. Reality was different—like it had always been. Henry, swallowed up by a job and a life that wouldn't allow them to be together.

"I hope we both get raises."

"Wow."

"Too soon?" Kit giggled and gave herself another twirl. "Okay, I'm going to find Henry in that crush of blowhards and see what we're doing next. How about you?"

"Uh, technically I'm off duty. I just wanted to know about the vote." Archie checked his watch. "I think I'll go back to my apartment—"

He was cut off when Kit's phone rang. Her private line.

"Hello? Henry! Congratulations! Can I have a puppy?" Kit enthused, then laughed at whatever her boss said. "Okay, cool. I'll tell him." She put her hand over the receiver and looked at Archie. "He's taking the limo up with David, but he asked if you could drive me."

"Oh, okay." Archie tried to play it cool. "Not a problem."

"He said yes. Do you want me to call up ahead? Food? Champagne?" She grabbed a pen and started to make notes. "Uh-huh. Uh-huh."

Archie got up to stretch his back and legs. He paced in a little circle around the reception space. Things were so different now. Maria and her desk were gone. Kit had rearranged the space—even gotten rid of the heavy drapes. It was light and open, inviting.

155

Kit hung up. "One more call and then we'll go. I got the rest of the day off to celebrate. Woo!"

"What can I do?" Archie chuckled at her enthusiasm.

"I'm supposed to tell you to tell your mom to please make apple scones."

Archie already had his phone out. "Done."

They busied themselves with arrangements for Henry's triumphant return home.

DAVID WAS waiting for him in the lobby, back straight and briefcase in hand. Henry strode out of the elevator, directly up to his godfather, eyes hard.

"We missed you at the celebration," he said, cool and easy.

With a handkerchief David mopped his forehead. "We'll have plenty of time to pop the champagne at the house. I had an important call to take." He leveled a glance at Henry, a small smile gracing his face. "Congratulations. You did it."

"Yes, I did."

He saw the limo pull up.

"Here's our ride...."

"Archie isn't driving us?" David asked as he followed Henry through the front doors, a nod to the doormen.

"He has the day off. I asked Paul to do it."

Frankly Henry didn't want David and Archie in the same small space; it was clear the two weren't going to get along anytime soon.

Which threw a wrench into Henry's plans right now.

He'd been thinking of a way to make things up to Archie, beyond a vacation when they could finally get away. What could he do to ensure them being together, as well as Archie's future?

The idea had come to him as he sipped champagne in that brightly sunny room.

It was such an amazing idea he didn't want to wait until they got home. He wanted to call Archie this instant and tell him. But no—no, the surprise would be better.

The ride to the estate was done in absolute silence. Henry checked his phone, scrolling through congratulatory messages and texts, the forwarded requests from the publicity department about press inquiries. Everything got a "Monday" in response.

He would talk to everyone on Monday.

The last text was from Archie.

Scones, really?

Henry swallowed a smile.

I'll share. Promise.

The response was quick.

Congratulations. You deserve this.

His fingers poised, Henry took a deep breath. Then he started typing.

Love you. We'll celebrate after everyone leaves.

It took twice as long to get a response, and every ticked-by minute made Henry anxious. Too much? Not enough?

Love you too.

Grinning, Henry leaned back against the seat and watched the world fly by.

Henry arrived home to a jubilant celebration, far different than the champagne and platitudes back in the boardroom. There were hastily tacked-up streamers in the formal dining room, something that made him laugh loudly as he stepped inside.

No one expected to find a balloon bouquet on a seventeenth-century sideboard.

There was a full spread of food and piping-hot apple scones on a cake pedestal in the center of the table. Henry felt his heart nearly bursting with love.

Libby gave him a happy hug. Evelyn pinched his cheek. Kit mentioned the puppy again, so he countered with a raise and got a hug in return.

So much for formal relationships between a man and his assistant.

Archie stood in the corner, almost shyly, until Henry couldn't wait a second longer. He headed over, hand extended—the twinkle in Archie's eye was charming.

"Congratulations. Siiiir." He used his old *Masterpiece Theatre* accent, much to Henry's delight.

"I think we should get you one of those formal chauffeur's uniforms. With a little hat."

"Kinky," Archie murmured under his breath as they shook hands vigorously.

"Come on and eat. I promised you could share scones."

Everyone enjoyed the meal and the champagne—everyone save David, who left three times to "take calls." When he came back the last time, he was smiling thinly but grabbed a glass of bubbly off the sideboard. He went to stand at the head of the table, eyes glittering.

"Here's to Henry—for winning over the black hearts of the board and taking his rightful place at WalkCom. Long live the king."

There was polite applause, then the raising of glasses, all in solidarity for Henry. This, he realized, clinking glasses with each of them, was his family. The people he trusted, the people he wanted around him in good times and bad. His gaze locked with Archie's, and suddenly he couldn't wait.

"Thank you, David." Henry stood up and took a deep breath. "I couldn't have done it without you. Without any of you. So thank you, from the bottom of my heart."

He blew out a nervous sigh. "A few announcements. I, uh, I wanted to say it's my great pleasure to announce my first official act as president and CEO—please allow me to introduce our newest vice president in the overseas operations department—Archie Banks."

Everyone turned to Archie with absolute surprise—which then became a joyful noise as Archie was quickly surrounded by well-wishers. Evelyn was crying, proud as could be.

Henry wanted to pat himself on the back.

"Interesting decision," came a low voice at his side. David was standing at his elbow. "Do you think it wise?"

"Yes, I do." Henry drained his glass of champagne. "He's smart, he's educated, he's worked for this family for years." He gave David a direct look. "I need people I can trust around me, David. I'm sure you understand that."

A war of unblinking stares waged momentarily; then David ducked his head. "Of course. I understand." He looked at his watch. "Must be heading home. Rebecca is waiting."

"I'll have Paul drive you."

ARCHIE ACCEPTED all the well-wishes and hugs with a plastered-on smile.

Vice president?

A simple job in the department would have probably rubbed him the wrong way, but being installed like that? A favoritism move. A move surely designed to bring him almost immediate disdain from every employee save Kit.

Fuck.

But he let his mother cry, and he accepted a friendly hug from Libby. It was easier to do this now.

He had to speak to Henry.

"Good evening, all. I'm taking my leave," David announced. He shot Archie a look.

Archie managed not to roll his eyes.

Libby offered to show him out, ever the hostess.

"Who wants seconds? Or are we up to thirds?" Evelyn asked, standing and examining what remained on the table. "More sweets?"

Henry settled into his chair, his smile wide and bright. "I can't say no."

They all ate a bit more, conversations quiet and of the chitchat variety as the stress of the previous few weeks made them all crave a lull. Archie kept trying to catch Henry's eye but to no avail.

Kit made noises about catching a train to get back to the city before it got too late.

"I'll drive you to the station." Archie twitched in his seat. He had to talk to Henry before his head exploded.

Finally, he couldn't wait any longer.

"Henry? Could I speak to you—alone?" he asked lightly, standing to convey his urgency.

Libby and Henry were deep in conversation; they looked up with surprise when Archie spoke.

"Of course." Damn, if his lover wasn't practically shining with warmth and happiness.

He hated having to do this.

Chapter Twenty-Two

Of all the things Henry imagined hearing after the kitchen door closed behind them, "What the hell was that?" was not it.

He turned to face Archie, frowning.

"What was what? I made it official. You're coming on board at WalkCom."

Archie's face didn't change. He still looked pissed.

"You didn't ask me."

"I wanted it to be a surprise!" Henry's frustration mounted. Was he not explaining this right? "You and I, working together. No sneaking around—"

"But still hiding our relationship," Archie cut in, stepping forward to stand just a few feet away from Henry.

That took him a second to respond to. "For now. Just for now," he said quickly, hands raised in front of him to try and stem the tide of Archie's protestations. "Just until things are back to normal."

Archie shook his head; the anger was quickly becoming sadness, and Henry's stomach dropped.

"Soon, though. I promise," he said softly, reaching out to touch Archie's arm. "Soon. You mean so much to me, and I swear, it will work out."

"Not if you're making decisions for both of us, Henry. And not if we're going back to the same routine. The same stupid rules." He sounded resigned, and that was far worse than mad.

"Fine. I rescind my offer. You're fired again." He tried humorous, but it fell flat. "We'll… we'll figure something out."

Archie nodded, clearly holding back some words. "I'm going to drive Kit to the train station."

"Paul can do that."

He shrugged. "I don't mind."

They stood in silence, the quiet tick of the wall clock their only soundtrack. Finally Archie roused himself. He leaned down to press a kiss to Henry's mouth, a gentle goodbye, but Henry had different ideas. He put his arms around Archie's neck and pulled him close, deepening the kiss until spots formed behind his eyes from lack of oxygen.

When Archie broke the kiss, a tiny smile tugged at the corners of his mouth. "Cheater."

"Hurry back. I want to negotiate your new position," Henry said, cheeky and breathless as he touched his fingers to Archie's mouth.

"That sounds dirty."

"Think filthy."

Archie reached around to slap Henry on the ass, then stepped out of the circle of their embrace. "You can't distract me with sex."

"Actually I can. Then, when you're half-asleep and pliant, I'll convince you to take the job," he quipped.

With a scowl—almost a teasing one—Archie turned and headed back out.

Henry sighed. Argument avoided. Or at least postponed.

When he reentered the dining room, everyone had cleared out. He followed voices to the foyer, where Kit was saying her goodbyes to Evelyn and Hilary.

"Everything okay?" Kit asked when Henry came over.

"Fine. Where's Archie?"

"Getting the car."

"Mrs. Walker's gone up to bed," Hilary said. "And I'm headed to my room unless there's something you need."

"No, I'll lock up once Archie gets back."

Evelyn patted him on the shoulder, and he leaned down to kiss her cheek. "Go on, you too."

"Come on, Evelyn. We'll watch a movie," Hilary coaxed.

"Hmmph," Evelyn said, but she gathered her cane and waved her good nights.

She and Hilary set off toward the servants' wing; the honk from outside made Henry and Kit chuckle.

"Tell him he forgets himself, and civilized people don't lean on their horn."

"Should I just flip you the finger in response now or let him do that when he gets home?" Kit asked drily.

Henry opened the door, ushering her out. He resisted the urge to wave at Archie, behind the wheel of the BMW this time.

When he turned to go inside, he caught a figure out of the corner of his eye.

David.

"I thought you'd left," Henry said, surprised. He closed the door behind him.

"Came back." David seemed a bit more disheveled than when he'd left earlier. His tie was gone, his jacket rumpled, his snow-white hair askew as if he'd been running his hands through it repeatedly. "We need to talk."

"Oh. All right. How about the study?"

"No."

Henry stopped in his tracks. His godfather's tone was strange. "Where, then?"

"Let's take a walk."

They went through the kitchen door, Henry following close behind as David walked along. He seemed to be moving with a purpose.

Twilight settled over the sculpted landscape; faint cricket sounds in the background. It was all a strange re-creation of the night before everything changed—sneaking out to meet Archie in the pool house.

He was caught up in the memory and missed David's movement, missed the swing in his direction—but he stepped out of the way, muscle memory and self-protection keeping him safe.

"What the hell?" Henry stood frozen as David transformed from disheveled old man to furious aggressor.

"Why are you doing this?" David spat out.

"Doing what?" Archie asked.

David paced back and forth along the footpath leading to the gate.

"Being so stubborn. You were supposed to let the board vote, let them vote you out!"

Henry stepped back, trying to puzzle through his godfather's words. "You told me to fight. You told me it was what my father wanted."

"Seriously? You develop a backbone now? That wasn't the plan, Henry."

A beat of silence.

"The plan?"

"After he changed the will, I knew I had to do something."

And the bottom fell out of Henry's world. Again.

"You were the one…."

David stopped pacing, shot Henry a bitter look. "Yes, me."

It was almost too much, and Henry felt a sick tickle at the back of his throat. The person his father had trusted—and loved—for so long. His closest friend.

"The kidnapping?" His voice was faint.

That withered David just a little; he shook his head, breathing heavily. "That wasn't supposed to happen. They—they took the money and completely deviated from the plan. You weren't supposed to get hurt—no one was."

"You killed my father." The words landed with a violent thud between them; David looked away, shoulders rounding.

"No—no. That wasn't the plan. He was just supposed to think Archie…."

A cold dread crawled over Henry's skin. "They were supposed to think Archie arranged the kidnapping. So my father would… what? Write him out of the will?"

What the hell did that paltry amount of money mean to David, who had millions?

"No, get rid of him. Get him away from you." David's gaze narrowed. "Leave you anchorless, alone. And get Norman to change his will—name me as CEO."

When Henry didn't say anything, David resumed his pacing. "He wanted you to have a choice. He wanted you to be able to walk away from the company." He stopped, eyeing the other man speculatively. "You still could."

"Why the hell would I do that? Besides—you're going to die in prison, you son of a bitch," Henry spit out. "No way you're getting anything now."

"Come on, Henry—take the money and your lover and run."

Henry's hands tightened into fists.

"He knew, Henry—he knew you were fucking that chauffeur of yours. He wanted you to be able to run away. Then he wouldn't have to worry about your pansy ass driving his empire into the ground."

ARCHIE FOUND the drive to the train station relaxing even as Kit chattered about the goings-on at the office.

"Lucy Galvins quit," she announced as Archie circled the parking lot, looking for a spot.

"David's assistant?" He remembered a pale woman who always wore ridiculously high heels.

"Yeah. Apparently he made a bunch of promises to her last year and then totally reneged."

Archie pulled the car into a spot in the far corner, then put it in park.

"Last year?"

"He told her he would be CEO at some point." She rolled her eyes. "And that meant she should work twice as hard—because there would be a big payout."

He turned out the car lights and unlocked the doors. "Why would he say that? Even if he knew about the will change, there's no reason to believe the board wouldn't pick Henry."

Kit shrugged. "No clue, but she was hopping mad when I saw her. Said something about suing or—and I quote—'something better than that.'" Her voice dropped conspiratorially. "I think he was boning her."

"TMI and something I don't want to envision." Archie pocketed the keys. "Come on, if you miss your train, I'm not driving you back into the city."

"Mmmmm, yes, I know. You need to get back to Henry." She all but laughed even as he froze.

When she saw the look on his face, she laughed harder.

"Seriously—you think no one knows?"

"Knows what? We're friends," he croaked. And he didn't even believe himself.

"Riiiight. With benefits." Kit opened the door, letting out a loud cackle.

"People know?" He scrambled out of the car.

"Yes. Not… everyone, but people know. I know. Hilary knows. Your mother totally knows." She slammed the door and hoisted her purse over her shoulder. "Libby knows. Hell, the aforementioned David Silver knows." She laughed.

Archie stopped walking and turned around to face her.

"How the hell did David know?"

Kit shrugged. "Lucy said he was bitching about it months ago. How you two were, uh… you know. Canoodling."

"I never heard about any gossip."

"Because there was none. Lucy told me, I said it was a bunch of crap, and it didn't go further." She continued walking toward the train platform. "I was trying to protect you both from rumors."

"Thank you," he said automatically, following her, numb down to his fingertips. "David never said anything to Henry."

"Why would he? It's private."

A memory niggled at him; the day of the will reading, David's reaction to the bequest made for him. He'd seemed annoyed at it, but the subsequent reactions to the clause about Henry had wiped that speculation away.

Now it made him wonder.

Why did David Silver care if Norman threw a few dollars his way?

HENRY'S HEART beat in triple time as David's words sank in.

His father wanted to give him the opportunity to leave WalkCom behind. Why would he do that? Did he really think Henry wasn't capable of running the company?

If that was true, a little voice said, why not keep the will as it was? Put David in charge.

Then he wouldn't be leaving it to chance.

And why give that money to Archie? It made no sense.

"Why do you think he was so hard on you, Henry? He knew! He knew you couldn't handle it." David pushed a little further, an edge of desperation in his voice.

Henry took another step back.

Norman didn't do subtle. He didn't manufacture drama.

If you knew him, you could interpret his actions.

"He was hard on me because he wanted me to be the best," Henry said, slow and deliberate. "He wanted me to have every opportunity in this world."

Even the one to walk away.

"If he didn't think I could handle the company, he would have said so. He would have… given it to you." A low blow, but Henry didn't even flinch. "He didn't do that."

David's whole body convulsed with anger.

"He gave me the chance to fight for it. And I won. Despite your interference."

The steroids. The infighting at the board meeting.

"He… he knew about Archie and me, and he…." A lump impeded his words. "He wanted Archie to get a good job; he wanted him to be free of debt. He wanted to give him a good start in this world."

So he could be his own man. Henry's partner, not his employee.

The revelation—whether it was fictionalized to get him through this horror or a true reading of his father's intentions—took Henry's breath away. He saw David in front of him, tense and vibrating with anger, and realized he was no threat. Not now, not before. Archie had saved him twice. And now Henry was saving himself.

"I'm going to call the police," Henry said quietly.

He turned on his heel, focused on the back door.

"No, Henry. You're not."

ARCHIE'S BRAIN whirred and clicked as he drove back to the house. Kit was off on the 8:15 to Manhattan, and Archie just wanted to get back to talk to Henry.

Something felt off to him. Something poking at his memory.

The FBI agent, in the hallway after Henry collapsed.

"Inside knowledge and a big bankroll don't necessarily equal results. Or maybe money wasn't what they were after."

David Silver wanted the CEO job—he expected the CEO job. The changed will was clearly something he knew about—and wasn't happy with.

The kidnappers didn't touch David.

They beat up Henry.

They shot Archie.

They even shoved Norman around.

They didn't ask for money.

They hid where they would be caught.

"Call 'Henry Walker cell phone,'" Archie said loudly as the car's computer system flashed lights on the dashboard.

He listened to the ringing as it passed "maybe he'll pick up in a second" and went to voice mail.

"End call. Call 'Walker estate housekeeper.'" Hilary's line. It would forward from the kitchen to her room after hours.

Four rings and Hilary picked up. He could hear the blare of the television in the background.

"Walker residence," she said crisply.

"Hilary? It's Archie."

"One second." The television's volume lowered. "Sorry about that. Evelyn and I are watching a movie. Everything all right?"

"Can you find Henry for me? It's important." He floored the gas as he approached the final stretch of road leading to the house.

"Sure. One sec."

The phone rattled as she put it down; he listened to murmurs of her conversation with his mother, then a door opening and closing.

"Archie? What's wrong?" Evelyn picked up the phone.

"Nothing, Mum," he lied, not at all surprised at the sound she made over the line. "I just need to talk to Henry."

"Hilary's gone looking for him."

"Mum, I have to ask you a question. About… Henry and I."

A small chuckle, and Archie shook his head. Of course she knew.

"Do you need my blessing, then? It's yours. It's been yours for years."

"Mum, please." He flushed with embarrassment. "Have you ever talked about—us—with anyone?"

"If you're asking me if I've gossiped." There was a warning there, and he paid it heed.

"No, I know you wouldn't. I mean—who have you talked to about your suspicions?"

"Weren't suspicions, as I was right."

"Mum."

"Fine. Me and Hilary have discussed it quite a bit, and I had a chat with Mrs. Walker a few weeks ago."

"That's it?"

"Oh, and hmmm."

Archie pulled up to the gates. He pressed the button on the dash to open them, waiting patiently.

"What?"

"Mrs. Silver said something the day of the funeral. I didn't pay it much mind, with so much going on. She asked if you were moving into the main house now, into Henry's quarters." She huffed a sigh. "Rude, if you ask me. So I played it off like I was daft—just said I didn't think Henry needed a bodyguard to sleep outside his door."

The gates opened slowly.

"I'm almost to the front door," Archie said, willing them to move quicker. "Is Hilary back yet?"

"No."

Archie cursed under his breath, then hung up with his mother. He sped down the driveway.

Chapter Twenty-Three

THE GUN in David's shaking hand was a surprise—a ridiculous one. The small, snub-nosed relic shook in his direction, leaving Henry stifling hysterical laughter.

He'd been menaced by men with automatic weapons. He'd been beaten up and watched his father lose his fight with a bad heart due to traumatic stress. This? This was almost insulting.

"I'm calling the police," he repeated, stepping backward now, keeping his eyes on David. "And you're going to lose everything."

"I could kill you."

"Of course you could. But that doesn't guarantee you anything, David. Not a damned thing. You have no guarantees the board will consider you as CEO."

The grass squeaked under Henry's shoes.

David stuck the gun out, aiming at Henry, or at least his general direction.

"You've known me my entire life," he said finally. "You knew my mother. How could you do this?"

The older man wavered—Henry could see his anger fluctuating with sadness and a defeated grief.

"I didn't mean for your father to die, Henry. I didn't. It wasn't supposed to be like this," he murmured. The gun shook in his hand. "I just wanted him to see… to realize…."

"David, please put the gun down. We need to end this now, before someone else gets hurt."

ARCHIE RACED up the steps.

The door opened; Hilary peeked out, a frown marring her features.

"What's wrong?"

"Henry and Mr. Silver are outside by the back door. I think they're arguing."

"Hilary, please take my phone and call Agent Feller at the FBI. Tell him I need to speak to him immediately." He pressed the smartphone into her hands, cupping them to hold it tight. "Tell him it's about Henry's kidnapping."

"Oh, of course." She looked as panicked as he felt, but took the phone.

He ran past her, down the hallway toward the kitchen, in a fast sprint.

"I'VE LOST everything," David whispered. The gun drooped a bit more; Henry took another step back, that much closer to the door.

"I'm sorry." Henry tried to keep his voice gentle, even as anger surged through him.

"I didn't mean it to happen."

"Of course not." The words were bitter on his tongue. David wasn't even looking at him anymore, so Henry quickly stepped onto the small stone patio. The pergola's beams were almost directly in front of him. Just a quick move to the left….

He heard commotion in the kitchen. The back door flew open, and Archie's unmistakable silhouette greeted him when he turned to see who it was.

"No, no!" Henry shouted, throwing himself toward his lover as he came barreling outside.

The shot exploded, and Henry flinched, expecting it to hit him in the back as he collided chest to chest with Archie. But there was just the sound and a whiff of gunpowder and Archie's shocked gasp as a thud echoed behind them.

When he looked, it was David on the ground, his face covered in blood.

Chapter Twenty-Four

Local police and agents from the FBI field office filled the foyer. Henry sat on the stairs, head in his hands, as he was peppered with questions.

So much violence. And for what? Money. Something he and David had far too much of to ever want for anything.

Stupid. A terrible waste.

"Mr. Walker?"

Agent Feller stood in front of him, ramrod straight from his shiny shoes to his neat-as-a-pin tie. None of them had slept; outside, the sun rose.

"What?"

There was no love lost between the two of them.

"Mr. Silver is out of surgery—apparently the shot didn't hit anything vital. They're expecting him to make a full recovery."

Henry shrugged. What should his answer be? His godfather, his father's closest friend—those men were a lie. At the very least they hadn't existed for some time. His machinations had killed Norman. He'd nearly orchestrated a mess that would destroy both Henry's and Archie's lives.

On a human level he didn't want David to die. Otherwise he didn't care.

"Good. Then he can give you a statement about how he was behind everything."

Agent Feller nodded stiffly. "We're in the process of searching his home and office."

"His assistant's name is Lucy. You might want to talk to her—apparently she has some axes to grind."

Henry rubbed his eyes with the palms of his hands.

"Thank you. Your statement…."

"That fellow over there. Maddox or something. He's got it." Tiredly, Henry checked his watch. "Is there anything else?"

"Can you come down to the local FBI office tomorrow?"

"Fine." Henry stood up, stretching and rolling his shoulders one at a time. "Ten all right?"

"Yes, thank you." Agent Feller clasped his hands behind his back.

Henry waited for an apology, then realized there wouldn't be one. Ever. Oh, someone from above the agent's head would contact him and use polite words to make nice. So he wouldn't sue.

But in the end their lives had been picked apart and accusations thrown, and nothing was ever going to make it better.

"Good night." Henry turned on his heel, then headed up the stairs to his room.

The commotion had kept the house in an uproar for hours.

Everyone had been roused from their rooms by the shot; Archie and Henry had done whatever they could to keep David alive until the ambulance came. Evelyn and Hilary made endless pots of coffee and tea for the scores of policemen and agents that swarmed around the house. Libby had called the security company, using harsh language until they sent people to watch the gates and keep the reporters away.

The Walker family needed their privacy more than ever.

He and Archie hadn't been able to talk since the police arrived. Yet again they were kept apart by propriety and station, and Henry—as he climbed the stairs—was done. Well and truly done.

Meet me upstairs was the text he'd sent to Archie after giving his statement to the detective.

Yes was the response.

It took him two hours to fulfill his end of the arrangement, but now he was entering his suite and shutting the door behind him with a sigh.

He was done.

"Henry?"

Archie came into the sitting room from the bedroom, a towel tied around his waist. He'd borne the brunt of the blood flow from David's head injury, stemming the flow with the sleeve of his jacket—a shower was mandatory.

"You okay?"

Henry laughed tiredly. "I am done."

"With?" Archie met him halfway, in the middle of the room.

"Drama. Lies." He tilted his head, searching the lines of Archie's handsome face for something. "Being kept away from you."

Archie's arms came around him, a tight embrace that made everything that wasn't in their little circle drift away. He slid his arms around Archie's trim waist, breathing in the warm scent of his bodywash on his lover's skin.

"I love you," he whispered into the curve of Archie's neck. "And I'm sorry I didn't discuss the vice president position with you beforehand."

"That really doesn't matter right now—the job thing. The love stuff is good to hear," Archie whispered back, trailing his fingers down Henry's side. He pulled at Henry's shirt, still tucked into his pants.

"I hereby formally rescind the job thing, but I'd like to formally request you become my boyfriend."

"Already am." Archie tugged at the shirt, slipping his hands underneath once he got it free. His hands felt heavenly on Henry's skin.

"Outside the bedroom." Henry exhaled, shuddering under the gentle touch of Archie's fingers. "In public."

"Huh." Archie traced up Henry's spine. "That... okay. Yeah."

The tremble in Archie's voice was the best thing Henry had heard in his life.

A TERRIBLE night morphed into something wonderful, at least to Archie. After Henry's declaration—request—Archie had undressed him gently, then ushered him into the shower. He went through another shower, unwilling to take his hands off Henry right now.

And reliving another moment of his life when he feared for Henry's safety.

When he'd come out to find David with a gun and Henry throwing himself into the possible path of a bullet, Archie's heart had stopped dead.

Watching David put the gun to his own head....

Archie'd already thrown up once tonight. He didn't want to repeat it.

They showered in silence, exchanging touches and kisses under the heavy spray. When the water began to cool, Archie shut off the taps—

then endured the terrible hardship of being pushed against the tiles and kissed senseless by his lover.

"You're incredible and you're mine," Henry murmured against his lips, rubbing their bodies together. "And I want everyone to know that."

Archie's heart sang.

They crawled into bed, pulling the covers over their heads.

"My father knew about us," Henry said softly, rubbing his forehead against Archie's shoulder. "He…"

"I know. Or I mean—I suspected it. When they read the will."

Henry nodded. "David confirmed it. It's why he changed the will in the first place." His voice shook slightly. "That's why David orchestrated the kidnapping."

The implications were loud in their tiny little cocoon. Archie wound their legs closer together, tangling his fingers in the hair at the base of Henry's skull.

"It's why he died…." Henry started, but Archie was quick to shake his head.

"No, no. He died because he had a bad heart and went through a horribly stressful experience. You had nothing to do with it. Nothing," he assured Henry. "I don't want you to blame yourself."

"Blame David," Henry whispered.

Archie nodded, pressing a kiss on Henry's forehead. "And think about the fact that your father knew and maybe approved. In his own way."

Henry swallowed, ducking so Archie was looking at the crown of his head.

"I think maybe he wanted me to know I could walk away, with you."

"You could," Archie murmured. "But I could also stay. With you."

"Yes. Please."

They were quiet for a long time until sleep flirted with Archie and Henry was breathing deeply against his arm.

THE NEXT thing Archie knew, he was awake and alone in the bed. Murmuring caught his attention—he moved the blankets off his head as he sat up.

Henry was at the door of the bedroom, in a robe, speaking to someone—Libby, from what he could make out. There was a second of panic, that he should be hiding or sneaking into the bathroom, but he made himself stay still. To see if Henry's resolution was going to stick.

"I have to go to the FBI office at some point," Henry said as he turned around. The door remained open a crack, with Libby—already fully dressed and made-up—framed in the doorway. She gave him a little wave. "We should probably get downstairs to eat beforehand."

It was all so casual. Archie smiled broadly.

"Give me ten minutes to get dressed."

"Perfect," Libby called. She patted Henry's arm before leaving.

Normal.

"I'm sorry I didn't ask. Are you okay with coming with me?" Henry shut the door, then fussed with the tie on his robe. He looked so young that Archie blinked, trying to reset his vision.

No, on second glance, he still looked younger.

"Of course." Archie threw off the covers. "Then I…. Do you want to go to the hospital?"

Henry paused, appearing to give it some thought.

"Maybe. I don't know yet."

"I'll ask you later."

They dressed, casual and comfortable, for the rest of the day. Paul had the stretch limo brought around; reporters were swarming at the gate, and he wanted something that kept out prying eyes. A second car, driven by a security guard, would follow and split off toward the city, hopefully dividing and conquering the paparazzi.

Their late breakfast was quick and quiet; Libby didn't join them, and Hilary was directing a cleaning crew around the house.

Evelyn shared coffee as they sat at the table.

"Like old times," she said as the men ate their eggs and toast.

Archie and Henry shared a look.

"I want grandchildren."

Archie dropped his fork.

They tried to be lighthearted, but there was no missing the men in white suits outside the back window, cleaning the blood off the ground. David Silver's attempted suicide and the revelations were weighing heavily on the house. Before they left, Libby met them by the door, worrying her hands.

"Henry? I just wanted to let you know... I've bought a ticket to Hawaii."

"Oh, okay." Henry reached out to touch her arm. "A little time away will do you good."

"I don't have a return ticket yet." She bit her lip. "I just... yes. Time away is what I need. Particularly now." The scandal was going to be insane.

Screwing decorum, he pulled her into a hug.

"Take care of yourself, okay? And know that your home is here, whenever you want to come back." The words tightened his throat; he cared about his stepmother, and he knew their shared grief was something that would always bind them together.

"Thank you, Henry. And please—come visit? You could use a vacation." She laughed wetly as she pulled away. "Both of you," she added, addressing Archie, who leaned against the door.

"I did promise him Hawaii," Henry said with a smile. He gave her one last squeeze.

"Terrific."

They exchanged more promises and goodbyes; Libby wouldn't be there when they returned.

It left them quiet as they slipped out of the house and into the limo.

Chapter Twenty-Five

IN THE end the visit to the FBI office was the easiest part.

The searches turned up confirmation of David's participation in the kidnapping plot, in the form of payouts and logistical information. Hired thugs, fortunately killed when the SWAT team rescued them at the motel.

Speaking to Rebecca Silver—and Lucy, the scorned assistant—filled in the blanks. All those visits to the house, no one questioning Henry's godfather being there whenever he wanted—easily dropping the steroids into whatever coffee or water Henry was distractedly living on while working.

Agents Maddox and Feller explained everything as Henry sat in a visitor's chair in Feller's office.

It was over.

They had all the answers to the investigative questions.

Of course nothing explained the "why"—why David had truly turned on his best friend and godson. When David woke up, maybe he would share. Or maybe they were doomed to never know.

Henry left the room to find Archie perched on the edge of an empty desk. He looked like a cat in a room full of rocking chairs, itching to be out of there.

"Come on," Henry said quietly.

"Where to?"

Henry considered where they could go. The estate was awash in bad memories, his apartment staked out by paparazzi. The office—God no. He would deal with that tomorrow morning—he'd called Kit and told her to send all but essential personnel home and have the public relations department handle the calls from the press.

For now....

"Let's go to your place."

The Heir Apparent

THE LIMOUSINE dropped them off three blocks from Archie's Lower East Side apartment. They seemed to have ditched the press tailing them. In the crush of locals and tourists, Archie and Henry were just two guys, holding hands as they walked down the street.

"Lunch?"

Henry shook his head. "I just want to enjoy this brief respite of non-notoriety."

They circled around, just in case, before arriving at the door of the small building Archie called home. He hadn't been home in days, evident by the overstuffed mailbox and stack of newspapers on the floor of the entryway.

They collected everything, then walked up to the fourth floor, where Archie's small studio was located. "We can order something later," Archie said, looking back at Henry as they climbed the stairs.

"Okay." He smiled up at Archie, tucking his hair behind his ear. "I've never been here before."

"I know, it's weird. So, uh—are you keeping your place? Or moving up to the house?"

Archie fiddled with the lock; Henry pressed against his back.

"I don't want to live at the house. I might stay in the corporate apartments for a while until the press dies down."

"Hmmm," he said, noncommittal.

The door opened; Archie pushed inside.

"Or buy a new place."

Archie turned on the lights, then threw the mail and papers on the kitchen table. "I'd offer you a tour, but this is it."

"We need a bigger place." Henry was standing in the middle of the room, near the foldout couch, framed by the large window behind him.

Trying not to smile, Archie sauntered over.

"Are you asking me to move in with you?"

"I could order you to but that would be rude." The twinkle in Henry's eye made Archie hot and bothered.

"It's kind of sexy."

"Huh. Then I demand you move in with me. And I also demand you fuck me right now."

"Yes, sir."

"ARE YOU going to come work for WalkCom?"

"No."

"Are you going to live with me?"

"Yes."

"Are you going to put up with my workaholic tendencies and the fact that I have no clue how to be a good boyfriend?"

"Yes. With the caveat that I will kick your ass when necessary."

"Deal."

"Are you going to love me forever and give Evelyn grandchildren?"

Henry's laughter and pink cheeks were suddenly the most treasured and beautiful things Archie could imagine.

"I love you," he said finally, touching Archie's smile with reverence. "Forever. We'll talk about the grandchildren in a few years."

"Okay, but you get to tell her that."

TERE MICHAELS unofficially began her writing career at the age of four when she learned that people got paid to write stories. It seemed the most perfect and logical job in the world, and after that, her path was never in question.

(The romance writer part was written in the stars—she was born on Valentine's Day.)

It took thirty-six years of "research" and "life experience" and well… life… before her first book was published, but there are no regrets (she doesn't believe in them). Along the way, she had some interesting jobs in television, animation, arts education, PR, and a national magazine—but she never stopped believing she would eventually earn her living writing stories about love.

She is a member of RWA, Rainbow Romance Writers, and Liberty States Fiction Writers. Her home base is a small town in New Jersey, very near NYC, a city she dearly loves. She shares her life with her husband, her teenaged son—who will just not stop growing—and two exceedingly spoiled cats. Her spare time is spent watching way too much sports programming, going to the movies and for long walks/runs in the park, reading her book club's current selection, and volunteering.

Nothing makes her happier than knowing she made a reader laugh or smile or cry. It's the purpose of sharing her work with people. She loves hearing from fans and fellow writers, and is always available for speaking engagements, visits and workshops.

Find her at:

Website: www.teremichaels.com
Twitter: @teremichaels
Facebook: www.facebook.com/tere.michaels.9

GROOMZILLA
TERE MICHAELS

When drama threatens to ruin a romance on a reality show, only a true friend can save a groomzilla's wedding.

Daniel Green, an event planner with a neat, quiet, orderly life, reluctantly agrees to plan the wedding of his childhood friend Ander, an outrageous fashion designer soon to marry a wealthy entertainment lawyer named Rafe. To complicate matters, the happy couple have agreed to have their wedding made into a reality show—something that practical Daniel isn't sold on.

Daniel is neither a romantic nor a wedding planner, but he's the only person in the world who can manage Ander. Distracting him from his mission is Owen Grainger, a too-handsome-to-be-true producer whose quiet charm pulls Daniel into his orbit.

When the stress of the show triggers bad behavior from Ander, co-producer Victor Pierce decides it's the key to a ratings bonanza, and he begins to undermine Ander and Rafe's relationship to create more drama. Daniel is determined to protect his friend and his own reputation, but when he finds himself falling hard for Owen, there's much more at stake than ratings.

www.dreamspinnerpress.com

THE VIGILANTE:
WHO KNOWS THE STORM

TERE MICHAELS

The Vigilante: Book One

In a dystopian near future, New York City has become the epicenter of decadence—gambling, the flesh trade, a playground for the wealthy. And underneath? Crime, fueled by "Dead Bolt," a destructive designer drug. This New City is where Nox Boyet leads a double life. At night, he is the Vigilante, struggling to keep the streets safe for citizens abandoned by the corrupt government and police. During the day, he works in construction and does his best to raise his adopted teenaged son, Sam.

A mysterious letter addressed to Sam brings Nox in direct contact with "model" Cade Creel, a high-end prostitute working at the Iron Butterfly Casino. Suspicion gives way to an intense attraction as dark figures from Nox's past and the mysterious peddlers of Dead Bolt begin to descend—and put all their lives in danger. When things spin out of control, Cade is the only person Nox can trust to help him save Sam.

www.dreamspinnerpress.com

THE VIGILANTE:
WHO KNOWS THE DARK

TERE MICHAELS

The Vigilante: Book Two

A wanted man after the destruction of the Iron Butterfly Casino, Nox Boyet must flee the island of Manhattan—the only home he's ever known. Together with Cade, Sam, and the rest of their ragtag group, Nox must find a place to hide from the District Police and the violent group of unknown drug dealers on his tail.

The solution—the Creel family farm in South Carolina.

But home isn't quite sweet for Cade, the prodigal son. As Cade struggles with his own secrets, shadows of the past threaten not only Nox's life, but his relationship with his son, Sam.

Nox knows there will never be peace unless he finds the answers to all his questions—and the answers lie back on the island. Cade and the others must choose their paths—find safety or follow the Vigilante into the darkness of the city? The city where Nox will come face-to-face with the past.

www.dreamspinnerpress.com

TERE MICHAELS

Faith &
Fidelity

Faith, Love, & Devotion: Book One

Reeling from the recent death of his wife, police officer Evan Cerelli looks at his four children and can only see how he fails them. His loving wife was the caretaker and nurturer, and now the single father feels himself being crushed by the pain of loss and the heavy responsibility of raising his kids.

At the urging of his partner, Evan celebrates a coworker's retirement and meets disgraced former cop turned security consultant Matt Haight. A friendship born out of loneliness and the solace of the bottle turns out to be exactly what they both need.

The past year has been a slow death for Matt Haight. Ostracized from his beloved police force, facing middle age and perpetual loneliness, Matt sees only a black hole where his future should be. When he discovers another lost soul in Evan, some of the pieces he thought he lost start to fall back in place. Their friendship turns into something deeper, but love is the last thing either man expected, and both of them struggle to reconcile their new and overwhelming feelings for one another.

www.dreamspinnerpress.com

TERE MICHAELS

Love & Loyalty

FAITH, LOVE, & DEVOTION: BOOK TWO

Faith, Love, & Devotion: Book Two

Seattle Homicide Detective Jim Shea never takes work home with him—until now. A judge banged his gavel, declared a defendant not guilty, and laid waste to a family. The emotional fallout of the trial leaves Jim vulnerable and duty-bound to the victim's dying father.

It's that man's story that screenwriter Griffin Drake and his best friend, actress Daisy Baylor, see as their ticket out of action blockbusters and into more serious fare. But to get the juicy details, Griffin needs to win over the stoic and protective Detective Shea. Their attraction is immediate, and Daisy encourages Griffin to use it to their advantage: secure the man, secure the story. Neither man has had much luck when it comes to love, and when their one night together evolves into a long weekend of rapidly intensifying feelings, both Griffin's fierce loyalty to Daisy and his very career is put to the test.

Because the more Griffin is drawn into a new life with Jim, the more his Hollywood life falls apart. Secrets and broken trust threaten Griffin's relationships, and he'll have to choose between telling the truth or writing a Hollywood ending.

www.dreamspinnerpress.com

TERE MICHAELS

Duty Devotion

FAITH, LOVE, & DEVOTION: BOOK THREE

Faith, Love, and Devotion: Book Three

A year after deciding to share their lives, Matt and Evan are working on their happily ever after—which isn't as easy as it looks. As life settles down into a routine, Matt finds happiness in his role as the ideal househusband of Queens, New York, but he worries about Evan's continued workaholic—and emotionally avoidant—ways. Trying to juggle his evolving relationship with Evan and his children, Matt turns to his friend, former Seattle Homicide Detective Jim Shea.

The continued friendship between Matt and Jim is a thorn in Evan's side. Jealous and uncomfortable with imagining their brief affair, Evan struggles to come to terms with what being in a committed relationship with a man means, and the implications about his love for his deceased wife, the impact on his children, and how other people will view him. His turmoil threatens his relationship with Matt, who worries that Evan will once again chose a life without him. But now, the stakes are much higher.

www.dreamspinnerpress.com

FOR MORE OF THE BEST GAY ROMANCE

Dreamspinner Press
dreamspinnerpress.com